"I wanted you from the minute I spied you through my binoculars. I wanted you before you even knew I existed."

"I did know you existed somewhere. I felt it," Billy said. "And when I bumped into you at the wedding, I knew I'd been waiting for you. I knew I'd see you again."

"That's because I put a spell on you all those days I had you in my sights," Mia said.

A thrill raced down his spine. Mia said the most unexpected things. He couldn't wait to get her in bed and discover all her other mysteries.

Suddenly, his phone rang. He didn't want this moment to end.

She put a hand against his chest. "You have to see who it is. In our line of work, we have to take calls—whether we want to or not."

He held up one finger. "Wait. Don't breathe."

Billy grabbed the intrusive device. Unknown.

He answered. "Yeah."

A woman's panting and sobbing assaulted his ears, and his heart banged against his rib cage. Could this actually be his sister?

MALICE AT THE MARINA

CAROL ERICSON

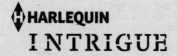

HARLEQUIN

INTRIGUE

HARLEQUIN®
INTRIGUE™

Recycling programs
for this product may
not exist in your area.

ISBN-13: 978-1-335-58241-6

Malice at the Marina

Harlequin Enterprises ULC
22 Adelaide St. West, 41st Floor
Toronto, Ontario M5H 4E3, Canada
www.Harlequin.com

Printed in U.S.A.

Carol Ericson is a bestselling, award-winning author of more than forty books. She has an eerie fascination for true crime stories, a love of film noir and a weakness for reality TV, all of which fuel her imagination to create her own tales of murder, mayhem and mystery. To find out more about Carol and her current projects, please visit her website at www.carolericson.com, "where romance flirts with danger."

Books by Carol Ericson

Harlequin Intrigue

The Lost Girls

A Kyra and Jake Investigation

Visit the Author Profile page at Harlequin.com.

CAST OF CHARACTERS

Billy Crouch—This hotshot LAPD homicide detective has been searching for his missing sister for five years, and just when he thinks the trail has gone cold, a mysterious woman shows up to give him hope...and heart.

Mia Romano—A US marshal who has lost her protected witness, she starts surveillance on the witness's brother, an LAPD homicide detective, and now she wants to get close to not only her witness but her witness's sexy brother, too.

Sabrina Crouch—She's been in witness protection for five years, but now it's time for her to call the shots in her own life, even if it puts her in danger.

Bri Sparks—She shows up in Billy's life to tell him his long-lost sister is still alive, but what is her motive?

Nick Carlucci—A member of the Carlucci crime family, he invited Sabrina to Vegas to get to know her and wound up falling in love...at his own peril.

Vince Carlucci—The leader of the Carlucci mob family has lost control of his brother, but he's willing to do anything to get it back.

Beckett—He works for the Carluccis, but his loyalty to one brother over the other just might get him killed.

Chapter One

LAPD homicide detective Billy Crouch gritted his teeth as he faced the toughest job he'd had to do in a while, his heart pounding, his mouth dry. He'd never felt less like his nickname, Cool Breeze, than at this moment. He patted his jacket pocket with a sweaty palm and blew out a short breath. He had all he needed to do the job.

When the music started, he shot a glance at his partner, Jake McAllister. J-Mac had had his back during shoot-outs, explosions and fistfights. Now it was Billy's turn to cover his partner.

He gave Jake a quick nod and stepped to the side as Jake's bride, Kyra Chase, resplendent in white lace and billowing veil, joined them at the outdoor altar. The arbor that arched over the happy couple sported flowers and seashells, and for one horrifying moment, Billy's nose tingled with an oncoming sneeze.

He sniffed, avoiding the catastrophe, and felt for the rings in his pocket one more time as if the mere thought of a sneeze could blow them away.

Billy listened to the vows in a blur, laughing in the

right spots and swallowing hard during the tender moments. If anyone deserved happiness, these two did. He leaped to his feet on cue and fished the rings from his pocket. As he handed them to the officiant, a chaplain from the LAPD, he squeezed Jake's shoulder.

Soon enough, the newly married couple floated down the aisle to claps and cheers, and Billy tipped his head back and forth, cracking his neck. Mission accomplished—until his speech.

The wedding guests bunched together as Jake and Kyra exited toward the beach for photos. As the best man, Billy would be joining them but didn't relish the thought of clomping through dry sand to pose for group pictures. Wet sand would be much worse, and he hoped Kyra didn't get any crazy notions about frolicking in the waves for the photo shoot.

As he wove his way through the crowd, two forces of nature barreled into him. He hugged his two sons, James and Darius, and then straightened their jackets. "You guys look sharp. Take those jackets off if you're going to run around."

Darius pointed to the waves crashing on the sand. "Can we play in the water?"

His older brother punched him in the arm. "Don't be an idiot."

Squeezing the back of James's neck, Billy said, "Don't call your brother names. We're not here for the beach, Darius."

"Can we go see J-Mac and Kyra?" Darius wriggled out of his jacket, bunching it between his hands like a soccer ball.

"Not yet. They need to take some pictures, but I know for a fact Kyra wants to dance with you." Over his sons' heads, he met his ex-wife's Sonia's gaze and tipped his chin in a short nod.

Her boyfriend, Nate, put his arm around her possessively. Billy felt like giving a brother a break, so he smiled at him. He didn't have a clue why the guy felt he had to prove something. Billy's marriage to Sonia had been over even before they separated. Sonia had tried her best, had given up her own career as a DA to raise the boys, but Billy was already married to his job.

Nate's company had relocated him to San Diego, and Billy had given his permission for Sonia to move down there with the boys. This was their first visit back to LA since the move. They'd been staying with Billy for a week before the wedding and would go back to San Diego tonight.

He missed them but didn't want to stand in the way of Sonia's happiness. Nate seemed like a good man, despite his insecurities around Billy.

He glanced down at Darius's scrunched-up face. "What's wrong?"

"Dancing? I'm not dancing." He kicked out at his brother, who was doing some silly moves in imitation of what he thought Darius might look like on the dance floor.

Billy tugged on James's earlobe and flicked Darius's nose. "You have to do what Kyra says—she's the bride. There's food under that tent. Don't touch anything you don't plan to eat, and you get one soda each."

James grabbed his little brother's arm, yanking him toward the white tent. "Yeah, right, Dad."

Billy shook his head and plodded through the dry sand to join the wedding party pictures.

Kyra broke away from Jake, her blond hair stirring in the sea breeze. She took both of Billy's hands and kissed his cheek. "You did a phenomenal job as best man."

"I guess J-Mac didn't tell you about the bachelor party." Billy winked.

"A bunch of cops talking about their exploits over some expensive Scotch?" She wedged a hand on her hip. "Heard all about it."

Thirty minutes later when the photo session wrapped up, Billy wandered back to the reception located on the rolling green lawn, the canopies of the tents flapping in the breeze like seagull wings. He dipped into the tent and snagged a plate, surveying the spread of crab cakes, shrimp cocktails, lobster rolls, beef satay, pork sliders, mini tacos, samosas, empanadas—a full array of food to reflect the diversity of LA. He stacked his plate and turned…right into a woman holding a champagne glass.

His elbow bumped her arm, and the bubbly coursed down the front of his rented tux jacket. Stepping back, he held his food aloft, not wanting it to join the champagne on his clothes, and brushed his hand against her bare shoulder to steady her.

"Whoa!" He glanced down into a pair of sparkling blue eyes.

The owner of those eyes flicked her dark hair over

her shoulder, tickling the back of his hand, and licked her fingers, still clutching the glass. "I'm so sorry. I was eyeballing those empanadas over your arm and wasn't paying attention."

Normally a stickler for his clothing, Billy dragged a napkin down his lapel and smiled. "No problem. Can I get you another glass?"

"Looks like I can take care of that myself." She crooked her finger at a roving cocktail waiter and snatched a flute from his tray. She raised it to Billy. "To the happy couple."

"To Jake and Kyra." He tapped his glass to hers. "Bride or groom?"

"Pardon?" She tilted her head, and a swath of mahogany hair slipped over one shoulder.

"Are you friends with the bride or the groom?"

She took a slug of champagne. "The bride."

"How are you acquainted with Kyra?" He knew Kyra didn't have family, but if she had a friend like this, she'd been holding out on him. Of course, Kyra had been instrumental in setting him up with the news reporter Megan Wright. It hadn't worked out between him and Megan, but they'd parted as friends on good terms. He hoped Kyra didn't hold that against him. Megan hadn't.

The woman before him coughed and waved a hand in the air. "Oh, Kyra and I go way back—childhood friends."

"My name's Billy, by the way." He held out his free hand after stashing his plate on the edge of the table.

"Nice to meet you, Billy." She took his hand briefly,

her fingers still sticky from the spilled champagne. "Sorry again about your jacket. I see some old friends. I need to mingle a bit."

Before he could ask her name or step aside so she could get her empanada, she floated away from him. Even though she wasn't as dolled up as most of the other women at the wedding, she had a spark that made her black slacks and flowy white blouse look elegant.

He put the stunning brunette out of his mind… for the time being. He had a more important task at hand. He ate his plate of food standing up and went over his best man's speech. He had a lot to say about Jake, not all of it fit for a wedding.

For the second time that day, someone bumped his arm, and he turned into a big hug from Fiona, Jake's teenage daughter.

"Isn't this the best, Billy? I love Kyra's dress and the beach and the food." She reached past him to grab one of the empanadas, which seemed to be attracting all the attention.

"Best wedding I've ever been to." He flicked his fingers against her champagne glass. "That's not the real thing, is it?"

"Dad said I could have one glass for the toasts. I'm just getting ready." She stuffed the empanada into her mouth, and flakes of crust stuck to her chin.

"Do me a favor." He lifted the flute from her hand and placed it on the table. "Go find the boys on the beach and make sure Darius isn't knee-deep in the ocean. You can pick up another glass of champagne when those toasts actually start."

"You got it, Detective." She saluted and wobbled off on her high heels, not yet practiced in walking on the grass with them.

Several plates of food later, his best man's speech delivered to raucous laughter and applause, and a few turns on the dance floor, Billy caught sight of the brunette who had run into him earlier.

He squinted as she made a beeline for the doors of the beach club that led to the parking lot. He felt a stab of disappointment all out of proportion to his brief run-in with...the woman. She hadn't even given him her name.

He rolled his shoulders. He could still ask Kyra about her childhood friend. As he raised his glass to his lips, his hand jerked and more champagne spilled on his jacket.

Kyra didn't have any friends from childhood. She'd been in and out of foster care for years, forming a close relationship only with the old LAPD detective Quinn. All of Kyra's friends were acquisitions from her adult life.

His gaze wandered toward the beach club. Could that woman have been a wedding crasher? Casual beach wedding, tempting spread, good music. She hadn't exactly been dressed for a wedding.

Billy snorted. That took some guts. He liked the mystery brunette even more now. He downed his champagne and headed toward the dance floor.

By the time Billy got home from the wedding, his

feet hurt from dancing and standing, and his face hurt from smiling. Jake had found his match in Kyra. Happy that still existed—for some.

Like Billy, Jake was divorced with a child who didn't live with him. Jake had had to fight his way back to a relationship with his daughter, Fiona, and Billy didn't plan on putting himself in the same situation with his boys. He wanted to be a part of their daily lives.

He hung his tux jacket on the back of a kitchen chair and grabbed a bottle of water from the fridge. He'd like to think that he and Sonia had gotten married too young and had grown apart. He didn't want to believe that his job precluded anything close to a happy relationship.

Didn't want to believe his sister's disappearance had cut him off from his emotions, either, although his marriage to Sonia had started heading south at about the time Sabrina went missing.

He downed his water and stripped off the rest of his tux. Dressed in a pair of gym shorts and a T-shirt, Billy snatched up his slacks and vest from his tux and hung them on the hanger in the plastic bag from the rental shop. He shook out the jacket and plunged his hand into the pocket to retrieve his best man's speech, even though he hadn't needed the paper. The speech had come from his heart, and he'd memorized every word of it.

He crumpled it in his hand and tossed it into the trash. If Jake ever got married again, Billy could bring it up on the computer. Grinning to himself, he patted the other pocket to make sure he hadn't left any cocktail napkins in there.

A piece of paper crinkled in the pocket, and he plucked it out. He smoothed it on the kitchen counter and read the words aloud.

"Don't believe everything you hear."

He rubbed his forehead. Nobody had to send that message to a homicide detective. He ran his thumb over the crinkled paper. Who *had* sent that message and why?

A guest at the wedding must've slipped it into his pocket, because he knew it hadn't been there when he dressed this morning. But why? Lots of cops had been in attendance. Was someone warning him about one of his cases?

He slipped the jacket onto the hanger and zipped up the garment bag around his tux. He had the murder of a tourist on his plate, along with a gang-style slaying. He'd assured Jake that he'd have them wrapped up before he came back from his honeymoon in Scotland.

Had he interviewed any witnesses whom he couldn't believe? And why not give him this warning directly? He knew cops sometimes got information in creative ways from sketchy sources who might not stand the smell test, but he and J-Mac didn't exactly have the reputation of sticklers. He'd consider a source, wherever it came from.

He went out to his balcony and gazed at the boats docked in the marina. He'd gotten close to plenty of people today, giving them the opportunity to put something in his pocket. Hell, he'd even left his jacket hanging on a chair while he hit the dance floor. Anyone could've slipped him that note.

As he stared at the water, a pair of dancing blue eyes floated into his vision. If anyone wanted to give him an anonymous note, it would be a stranger—a stranger who didn't give him her name and lied about knowing Kyra.

Had the mysterious brunette crashed the wedding to give him that warning?

If so, it meant he'd see her again, and he hadn't looked forward to seeing someone again as much as this in a long time—wedding crasher or not.

Chapter Two

Mia Romano squinted at the tall silhouette of Detective Billy Crouch on the balcony of his Marina Del Rey condo, and her heart did a little flip-flop. The surveillance photos had already made her think of Idris Elba and a young Denzel, but she hadn't expected the full force of his hotness to bowl her over and almost ruin her cover. She fanned herself with her hand, despite the sharp breeze whistling from the water.

Billy and his wife had sold their home in Ladera Heights as part of the divorce, and he'd rented this place while looking for a suitable replacement home for him and his two boys when they came to stay. She knew his nickname, his two current homicide cases, how long he'd been on the force, his most recent girlfriend, his tailor where he had his suits custom-made, but damn, she didn't know seeing him in person would hit her like a ton of bricks. Maybe he'd had such an impact on her because she knew more about him than she'd known about her ex-fiancé.

She sniffed and pulled her hoodie around her body. The summers in LA were toasty, but nighttime on the coast always brought a chill to the air, even without the presence of the marine layer.

She gazed past the masts of the sailboats bobbing against their slips, halyards clinking out a rhythm in time to the water lapping against the sides of the boats. The absence of fog tonight made her job a little easier, and she eased the binoculars from her backpack.

She swung them upward to zero in on Billy's balcony, but he'd gone back inside. A kernel of disappointment lodged in her belly. She could've watched him all night long.

She dropped her sights to the entrance of his condo complex. A couple hovered at the door, their heads together, and Mia sharpened her focus.

The woman had her hand on the man's chest at arm's length as the man gestured with his arms. Mia murmured, "Give it up, dude. She's not inviting you inside."

They eventually broke apart, and the woman slipped through the glass door without one look behind her. The man stomped off, and Mia watched him leave. A little drama, but not connected to Billy.

The engine of a small boat puttered in the distance, and Mia tracked the source. A motorized skiff chugged along the channel, cruising past the slips. The skipper cut the engine across from Billy's building, and a figure stood in the boat facing Billy's balcony. The small craft bobbed in the water for several more minutes, and then the engine sputtered back to life and the boat did a U-turn in the channel.

The blood in Mia's veins thrummed. Too bad she didn't have a boat to give chase. She followed the boat's progress to the end of the line of slips before it disappeared from her vision.

Mia lowered her binoculars and tucked them into her backpack. She slid behind the wheel of her car, tossing her backpack onto the passenger seat. She wheeled out of the parking lot and pulled onto the street that sat at the top of Billy's cul-de-sac. If any car ventured this way, she'd see it, photograph the license plate and catalog it—just as she'd been doing for the past week once they got word of Chanel's departure.

She retrieved the thermos from the floor of her car and poured some hot coffee into the silver cup. She blew on it before taking a small sip. She'd better reserve some for the long night ahead.

A few minutes later, her cell phone buzzed in the cup holder. She tapped it, along with the speaker button. "Hey, Tucker."

"Did you make contact today, Romano?"

"I did. I crashed the wedding."

"Do you think he'll remember you to be open to another chance encounter?"

Mia clutched the steering wheel for a few seconds, recalling how Billy's dark eyes had probed hers. How his hand seemed to caress her shoulder as he steadied her when she bumped into him. How his gaze burned into her back when she walked away from him.

"I think I made enough of an impression." She neglected to tell Tucker about the note she'd slipped into

Billy's pocket. She'd been all for approaching Detective Crouch with the facts, but she'd been overruled.

"Okay, good. Get close to him. Find out what he knows." Tucker coughed. "You still on surveillance?"

Mia flicked a finger at her half-full thermos of hot coffee. "For the rest of the night."

"Then I'll let you get to it."

Tucker ended the call, and Mia took another sip from her cup, lolling the dark roast on her tongue before swallowing it. Getting close to Billy Crouch would be a definite perk of this assignment.

Mia caught her breath as a shadow moved along the sidewalk in front of the condo complex. She pulled out her binoculars and scanned the area where heavy foliage spilled onto the concrete. The image flickered again and disappeared.

The figure seemed to be hugging the bushes, stepping onto the sidewalk when necessary. Not a typical evening stroll or dog walker. Could be the homeless person she'd seen in this area before.

Only one way to find out. Mia killed her dome light and eased open the car door. She slung her pack over one shoulder and clicked the door shut.

On silent feet, she crept to the sidewalk and followed a dirt path next to the pavement. Occasionally, the bushes grew close to the sidewalk, forcing her onto the concrete. She followed the same path as the shadow, even saw the areas where the person ahead of her had tracked dirt onto the sidewalk.

Billy's condo lay another twenty yards ahead, and she'd lost sight of the dark figure. Had the person made entry into the building?

Mia hunched down as she approached the break in the foliage that signaled the entrance to the condo complex. The lights from the lobby spilled through the glass doors, creating a solid bright path to the sidewalk. Mia poked her head around the edge of the bushes, taking a quick peek into the lobby and an expanse of brass mailboxes. A woman in pink bunny slippers and flannel pajama bottoms glanced up from the mail in her hands, sensing Mia's presence outside or perhaps seeing her shadow.

This woman was not the figure Mia had been tracking. As Mia turned, leaves rustled and twigs snapped deep in the landscaping that curved around the building.

Mia ducked beneath a tree, tripping on an exposed root. Swearing, she grabbed the tree trunk to keep from falling. As she straightened up, she spotted a figure in dark clothing slipping over a stucco wall.

Mia clambered through the bushes, leaves sticking to her hair and twigs clawing at her clothing. She grabbed the top of the wall and hoisted herself up just in time to see the black-clad figure running toward the boat slips. Seconds later, the sound of a putt-putt engine echoed over the water.

Mia released the wall, her sneakers hitting the soft ground. Someone else had been on a reconnaissance mission tonight. She rubbed her palms against the thighs of her jeans.

Seemed she wasn't the only one who wanted to get close to Billy Crouch.

TWO DAYS AFTER the wedding, Billy pulled out of the parking lot of LAPD's Northeast Division in his unmarked sedan. He'd just slogged through the first day of what would be a long three weeks without his partner. Jake and Kyra must be in Edinburgh now, the first stop on their honeymoon. No couple deserved that happiness and peace more than Jake and Kyra, so Billy would try to contain his self-pity.

He'd outdone himself with the grocery shopping when the boys were with him for a week and even managed to cook some pasta and steaks for dinner, but now he faced bare cupboards and an empty fridge. He made a detour off the Marina Freeway to swing by his favorite Chinese take-out place.

He parked in the strip mall parking lot on Lincoln and shuffled into the line for the crowded restaurant's counter.

As he checked his phone, someone bumped his arm. He turned and looked into the smiling eyes of the wedding crasher.

She held up her soda. "Thought you might want to add some soda to the champagne."

Billy's mouth dropped open, but for once in his life, no words came to his lips. Had she followed him here? He glanced at the drink in her hands. She'd already ordered, so she must've been here before him.

Her dark brows created a V over her nose. "I'm sorry. It is you, isn't it? The best man from the wedding in Malibu this past weekend?"

"Yes, yes." He patted his chest. "That's me, but what are you doing here? Malibu to Marina Del Rey? That's some coincidence."

She tilted her head and wrinkled her nose. "They're both on the coast, aren't they? I know. I couldn't believe it when I ordered and then saw you standing in line. Billy, right?"

"You got it, but you never told me your name." He fished in his jacket pocket for his wallet as he moved closer to the counter.

"Shh. Don't tell anyone, but I kind of crashed that reception." She held a finger to her lush lips, painted with a deep rose lipstick.

"I figured that." He laughed, feeling better than he had all day without his partner. "The bride doesn't have any friends from childhood."

She smiled. "I didn't expect to get busted."

She'd stayed with him in line and now stood to the side as he ordered some kung pao beef, orange peel chicken and fried rice.

When he finished his order, she put her hand on his arm. "Order it for here. I was going to eat on the patio outside. You can join me…if you like. I mean, if you're not in a hurry."

"Uh…" Billy took the paper cup the counter person offered. "I'm not in a hurry. I'll get my drink and meet you on the patio."

"Perfect." The brunette twirled around and headed for the front door.

Billy had a surreal moment when he thought he'd imagined the entire encounter and she'd walk right out of his life again. But after hurriedly filling his cup with ice and Coke and sailing out the front door, he spotted her at a table in the fenced-off patio area.

She waved to him and he practically flew to her table. He pulled out the plastic chair across from her and sat.

"Let's start over." He held out his hand. "I'm Billy Crouch."

She took his hand, her blue eyes giving him her unwavering attention. "I'm Molly Jones, full-time Realtor, part-time wedding crasher."

"Realtor, huh?" He squeezed her hand before releasing it. "I might need your services."

Cocking her head, she held up one finger. "Hold that thought. I just heard my order number over the speaker."

Molly jumped from the table, nearly knocking her chair to the ground. She righted it before charging inside the restaurant.

At least he'd gotten her name this time. Now he needed to find out what she was doing in Malibu at the time of Jake's wedding.

She returned with a red tray and a plate piled high with beef and broccoli, some entrée with chicken, a mound of fried rice and a couple of spring rolls. She'd ordered more than he'd ordered. Maybe she had an insatiable appetite, and that was why she crashed the reception—although she hadn't even grabbed that empanada.

Flicking a napkin at her plate, she said, "I think I went overboard."

"Dig in. You don't have to wait for me." Billy shook the ice in his cup before taking a sip.

She pinched a spring roll between her chopsticks and held it up. "Have some of mine before you pick up your food."

"You're sure?"

"I don't need two of these with the rest of this food staring me down."

He took the chopsticks from her fingers and crunched into the crispy shell. He rolled his eyes to the sky. "So good."

"I'm not going to sit here and take your word for it." She picked up the other spring roll with her fingers and took a bite, a tiny shred of cabbage clinging to her lips.

Food on someone's face had never looked so good. He started when he heard his number over the speaker, and he placed the chopsticks on a napkin. "I'll use these and get you another set."

Even more people had crowded up to the counter to order and pick up their food. Billy waved his receipt in the air. "Number forty-two."

He squeezed in next to a man arguing with the employee. The guy raised his voice. "I ordered it. I don't know where my receipt is. Beef and broccoli, some spring rolls…"

Billy grabbed his tray and shouldered past the irate

customer. When he got to the table, Molly had finished her spring roll and was sipping her soda. He dropped the extra chopsticks next to her plate. "These are for you."

"Thanks." She tapped the chopsticks on the table to remove the paper.

Billy nudged his plastic chair with his foot and took his seat across from her. "Some guy at the counter was having a fit over his missing order."

"It *is* crowded. He should cut them some slack." Molly pushed the rice around her plate with her chopsticks and nibbled on a piece of chicken. "So, that was a cop wedding or something? I overheard a lot of cop conversation and figured I'd picked the wrong wedding to crash."

"Yeah, cop wedding." Billy pointed the chopsticks at his chest. "I'm a detective with the LAPD."

"Uh-oh. I knew you were trouble." She winked at him. "Definitely should've picked a different wedding."

"Why *did* you crash it?" Billy dug into his food, that wink almost turning him into a drooling idiot.

She shrugged. "I was supposed to meet a client at the beach club, and she didn't show up. I saw the festivities out the window and decided to check it out on a whim. I don't usually barge into other people's events like that, but it looked so magical."

"You have another client out this way?" He waved his chopsticks in the air.

"A few, but I actually live here." Molly puckered her lips around her straw and met his gaze over the cup.

"So do I. Condo?" The coincidences were beginning to pile up. It was fate…or something.

"What else, around here?" She pushed her plate away and dug her elbows into the table. "How long have you been living in the marina?"

"Less than a year." He raised his left hand and flicked it back and forth to show her his left ring finger. "Divorced. Are you married?"

She repeated his gesture, flashing a turquoise ring on her left finger. "Nope. Came close once. Dodged a bullet."

"Was the bullet the marriage or the guy?" He patted his mouth with his napkin. He'd gotten more personal with Molly in just a few minutes than he had with any of the women he'd dated, post-separation. Had he turned a corner, or did the detective in him signal a need to know more about this woman?

He said, "If that's too personal, you don't have to answer."

"Oh, definitely the guy. I'm not anti-marriage, but it's best if you stick with a partner on the right side of the law."

Billy's eyebrows shot up. "Was your fiancé a criminal?"

"Well, I had to learn my wedding crashing skills from someone." Her phone buzzed on the table, and she lifted one edge and peeked at the display. "Clients. I do need to get going. Can I give you my card? In case you're ready to move out of that condo."

"Absolutely, as long as I can call you even if I'm not ready to move."

She glanced up from digging in her purse, and her blue eyes smiled. "I'd like that, Billy."

She pinched a white card between her fingers and snapped it on the table next to his plate. "Anytime."

Toying with the edge of the card, he read her name, number and a realty company he'd never heard of. "You're not affiliated with any of the big companies?"

"My partner and I run a boutique agency. More money for us, but more personalized service for you." She pushed back from the table and hitched her bag over her shoulder. "I'm so glad I ran into you today... and that you didn't arrest me for being an interloper on your friends' big day."

"Glad I met you, too, Molly." He pointed at her plate, where she'd left all of her beef and most of her chicken and rice. "You don't want to take that with you?"

"Oh, no." She patted her flat stomach. "I ordered way too much. Call me, Billy."

He raised the finger he was pointing to her food with and formed it into a gun as he leveled it at her. "Count on it."

Her smile faltered for a second before she turned and left the patio, her dark hair swinging behind her, her hips matching its sway.

Billy narrowed his eyes as he watched her back. Nothing seemed right about that woman, except his attraction to her. He pocketed her card and scooped up another mouthful of kung pao beef and rice.

He'd have to get up close and personal with her to discover what she really wanted...and he was looking forward to it.

SEVERAL HOURS AFTER the unexpected dinner with the mystery woman, Billy collapsed on the couch, his laundry done, his floor mopped, his FaceTime negotiation between his warring sons successful. He grabbed the remote and engaged the recliner.

As he navigated to the British cop show he'd been watching, a knock on his door echoed through the partially furnished living room. He swore under his breath, forgetting for a second that he could do that out loud with the boys gone. Some moron must've let someone into the complex, or a solicitor tailgated their way into the building. He'd warned his neighbors about it several times.

He paused the show and walked toward his front door. His pulse ratcheted up a few notches, thinking that Molly had somehow tracked him down again.

He leaned toward the peephole, and a young woman stepped back as if she knew he had her in focus. He swung open the door, and she jerked her head up, the colorful beads in her braids clacking with the movement.

"Oh." Her mouth formed an O, matching the word.

"Can I help you?" The young woman reminded him too much of his sister for him to take a hard line with her. Maybe she just had the wrong place.

"A-are you Billy Crouch? The LAPD detective Billy Crouch?"

Billy's muscles tensed, and he had a fleeting thought that he should have tucked his weapon in his waistband before answering the door. "*You* knocked on *my* door. Who are you?"

She took a big breath, her shoulders dropping. "Yes, I'm sorry. My name is Bri."

"Doesn't mean much to me." He tightened his grip on the doorjamb and glanced past her down the hallway in case she had an accomplice. "Again, can I help you?"

"Oh, no." She shook her head back and forth, sending her beads into another song. "It's me who can help *you*."

Billy cocked his head. Was this some kind of come-on? "Explain or move along."

"I know your sister, and I can help you find her."

Chapter Three

That familiar rush of hope flooded his body, and Billy widened his stance to keep his balance. He crossed his arms, wanting to believe but not eager to go down the road of false hopes again. "How do you know my sister? What's her name? What does she look like?"

Bri glanced over her shoulder. "Can I come in?"

Inviting her in would reduce the likelihood that she had some accomplice waiting in the wings, so Billy swung open the door. "Come on."

She squeezed past him, clutching her bag to her chest. "Your sister's name is Sabrina. She's tall, like you. Maybe five foot eight, slender."

"Go on." He slammed the door. She'd nailed it so far.

"She wears her hair different ways. Last time I saw her, she had natural curls, about shoulder length." She held out her slim brown arm, sinewy with lean muscle. "Her coloring is a little darker than mine but lighter than yours."

Billy wedged a shoulder against the door. He could see his sister with that hair style. "That describes a lot of Black women."

Bri licked her lips. "She has a tattoo on her right shoulder blade."

"Sabrina doesn't have a tattoo." Billy's shoulders slumped.

"A tattoo of a dolphin."

"A dolphin?" Billy gulped. Sabrina had always loved dolphins ever since he took her whale watching and a school of them had followed their boat, arcing gracefully out of the water and frolicking in the waves. He took a deep breath. "Sit down, Bri."

She put a hand to her chest as she perched on the edge of his couch. "Thank you. Y-you haven't heard from her, have you?"

"Me?" Billy widened his eyes. "I haven't seen my sister in over five years. Tell me what you know."

"I knew Sabrina in Vegas." Bri clasped her hands between her knees. "She got in with a bad crowd. Her boyfriend was abusive."

Billy flinched and clenched his hands into fists. "Why didn't she call her family? Why did she disappear in the first place?"

"I'm not sure about that part." Bri worried the skin at the side of her thumb with her teeth. "I didn't meet her when she first got to Vegas…only later when she was with Lawrence."

Billy etched the name Lawrence across his brain. He'd get the rest of this scumbag's details later, and then he'd… "Why are you here now? When did you last see Sabrina?"

"She left Lawrence, took off without telling anyone."

Squeezing the bridge of his nose, Billy said, "Seems

like that's a pattern. So, you think she left Lawrence and came here?"

"She'd mentioned her brother was a cop with the LAPD. That's how I found you. I… I sort of followed you from the station. I figured she might come to you for help."

"Why now? Why not anytime in the past five years?" He slammed his fist into his palm, and Bri jumped.

"Because she was with Lawrence. She didn't want you to know about their relationship. As far as I know, she went to Vegas because of Lawrence. She knew you'd disapprove, and then she just got in so deep with him she couldn't leave." Bri lifted her shoulders.

"How'd she get to Vegas in the first place?" Billy ran a thumb across the creases in his forehead. "She didn't take her car. It was parked in a shopping center near the airport. We couldn't trace her phone after that point. She'd turned it off. No credit card or banking activity, either. What did she do? Hitchhike to Vegas?"

Bri spread her hands, and her long fingernails sparkled with glitter. "I can't help you with that part. She never told me how she did it. Just that she'd left LA for Vegas and hadn't told her family."

Billy sank his head into his hands. Why would Sabrina want to torture her family like that? Keep them in the dark? All for an abusive guy? Dad had passed away during those five years, probably from a broken heart more than anything, and Mom had moved in with her sister in Mississippi.

He glanced at Bri, who studied him with tears shimmering in her dark eyes.

"I know this is hard for you, but Sabrina is a good person. She got in over her head. She loves you, but she thought you'd be judgmental."

"Me? Judgmental?" Billy jumped from the chair and paced to the window overlooking the boats in the marina.

Sabrina could do no wrong in his mind, but had he put her on a pedestal? He'd risen quickly through the ranks of the LAPD after a stint in law school, the perfect wife, the house in Ladera Heights, the custom clothes. Did she see all that and believe he expected the same from her? Had he?

He spun around. "What now? Why come to me? I'm clearly not her go-to guy."

"I think you may be now. I believe she's going to contact you. Maybe not directly, and that's why I'm here. That's why I want to help you. She's afraid of Lawrence and his crew." Her gaze darted toward the sliding glass door to the balcony. "They may even be watching you to find her."

"You think she's going to try to contact me on the sly? What's Lawrence's last name? What's your last name?"

She blinked rapidly. "Honestly, I don't want to tell you my last name."

As he leveled a finger at her and opened his mouth, she cut him off. "But Lawrence's last name is Coleman, and I swear I will help you if Sabrina tries to contact you. I can keep a look out for his Vegas homeboys. I should know… I dated one."

Billy stopped pacing and gave her a sharp glance. "Are you safe? Do you want something to eat or drink?"

"I'm fine, but I need to leave now." She swept her bag up from the floor and pushed to her feet. "I know how to contact you. I'll be in touch, so if anything happens out of the ordinary, anything at all, let me know. I might be able to link it to Sabrina."

He walked her to the door, and she paused in front of it before he opened it for her. In fact, she hadn't touched anything in his place since she got here. He recognized the tactics of someone not wanting to leave prints. He'd check the video footage of the condo complex and see if she'd touched anything on her way up here.

As she walked toward the elevator, she cranked her head over her shoulder. "I'll be in contact. Have faith."

She punched the button with her knuckle, and the doors closed behind her.

After he shut his front door, he stood against it for several seconds. He'd been so busy verifying Bri's information and asking questions, he hadn't given himself time to celebrate this news. Sabrina alive? On her way to LA? He couldn't be disappointed again.

Bri had asked him to note anything out of the ordinary. He stroked his chin. Was it out of the ordinary to run into a woman lying about knowing the bride at a wedding and then seeing her again a few days later, fifteen miles away from that wedding, at a Chinese restaurant?

Billy picked up a book he'd been reading and shook the piece of paper he'd been using as a bookmark from between the pages. He ran his thumb across the crinkled words.

Don't believe everything you hear? Right now, he didn't believe anything he'd heard from anyone.

MIA LEVELED HER binoculars at the young woman who slipped out of the front doors of Billy's building, her beaded braids swinging as she sashayed down the sidewalk. She walked with a mission-accomplished air. But what was her mission? Was she the same person in the boat?

When Mia had spied Billy at his window, it seemed as if he'd been talking to someone. Although Mia hadn't spotted the young woman inside Billy's place, the timing from when she'd seen her piggyback into the building to Billy's appearance at the window matched. Watching the woman hop into a silver compact parked at the curb, Mia sawed her bottom lip with her top teeth. She could just be a friend. Maybe a lover.

"Too young for Billy." Her own loud voice in the confines of the car startled her. After studying Billy's background, she knew his type—accomplished, smart, savvy and close to his own age. Of course, it could all be wishful thinking on her part. She'd have an easier time drawing close to Billy if he were single—a purely professional interest.

She snorted as she tossed her binoculars on the passenger seat and slumped down as Billy's visitor made a U-turn and headed toward her stakeout position at the end of Billy's street. The headlights of the compact flooded her car for a second, and Mia waited a few more seconds before pulling out behind her at a safe distance.

In this mostly residential area with access to the marina, cars still dotted the streets. One more car behind her shouldn't alert the woman to anything special.

When she turned onto busy Lincoln Boulevard, Mia dropped back a few cars and shifted to the right-hand side of the lane to keep the small silver car in her sights. When the car pulled into the left-turn pocket for Washington, Mia followed suit. The busier, the better. But a turn onto commercial Washington probably meant the woman wasn't going home.

A block later, the compact jimmied into a small space on the street with metered parking. Mia had no such luck but didn't want to lose sight of the woman by circling around trying to find parking. She idled at a green curb, her gaze following the woman into a bar with people spilling onto a patio in the front.

Mia cranked her wheel and crawled down a side street, reading the parking signs—all resident permitted parking. She blew out a breath. She either risked getting a parking ticket or risked missing Billy's visitor by wasting time driving to the public parking lot. She gripped the steering wheel and slid into a spot between two SUVs. This counted as a business expense, didn't it?

She hiked back to the main drag. She drew abreast of the silver compact and crouched down, pretending to tie her boot. As she rose, she attached a GPS tracker to the underside of the car—just in case she missed her mark tonight.

The music from the bar with the open patio thumped onto the street, and Mia ducked inside. She blinked several times as her eyes adjusted to the low lights. She zeroed in on the woman hanging on to the bar, leaning toward the bartender, her braids swinging inches from the mahogany.

Mia sidled next to her and waved at the bartender. "Can I get a beer?"

He ignored her and hustled to the other end of the bar to pour a couple of glasses of wine and dump some ingredients into a blender.

Mia caught her quarry's eyes and shrugged. "Crowded in here."

"Uh-huh." She flicked a braid over her shoulder, her gaze shifting to the front entrance.

Mia tried again. "Is it always this busy?"

"I don't know. Never been here before." The woman didn't even meet Mia's eyes when she answered.

She'd bet anything this woman hadn't been this standoffish with Billy.

The bartender returned with a fruity drink and placed it on the cocktail napkin in front of the woman. "That's nine bucks. You wanna run a tab?"

The woman sucked on her straw and raised her dark eyes. "I'm meeting someone. Can you use his card when he gets here?"

"Doesn't work that way." He wedged his hands on the bar, tattoos winding up his beefy arms. "You can pay for this drink now or leave me a card to start a tab. When your friend gets here, I can switch the cards."

Her liquid brown eyes darted toward the door again, and then she pulled out a credit card and snapped it onto the bar.

Before the bartender could grab it, Mia snatched it up and glanced at the name on the card. She extended it between two fingers to Brianna Sparks.

"That's okay. I'll pay for her drink if you can just get me my beer."

Brianna's eyes widened, and she clutched her glass as if she were afraid Mia would take it from her.

The bartender glanced from Mia to Brianna and shrugged. "Whatever. What'll you have?"

Brianna breathed out a thank-you and then slid from her stool to cross to the other side of the room.

Mia ordered a bottle of light beer and swiveled around to see who Brianna was so anxious to meet.

The young woman practically skipped up to an older white guy, shaved head, smooth dresser. He cupped Brianna's elbow and steered her to a table crammed in a corner.

Mia had no hope of eavesdropping on their conversation or getting close to Brianna again, but at least she'd gotten her name from her credit card. She perched on her stool sideways to keep an eye on the couple.

When Brianna tipped her head toward Mia and the man's beady stare followed, Mia spun back toward the bar and hunched over her beer. Had she been made?

Had the man asked Brianna if anything unusual had happened, or had she just offered up that an overly friendly woman at the bar had bought her drink?

In either case, she couldn't do anything more tonight. She shoveled some of the bar's pretzel mix into her mouth and took another swig of her beer to wash it down.

She dusted the salt from her fingers and grabbed her purse from beneath the bar. Brianna's friend had made his way to the restrooms a minute before, and Mia chanced a final look at Brianna on her second fruity drink of the evening, her head bent over her phone.

Once outside, Mia took a deep breath of the slightly salty air and strode down the sidewalk to her car. She turned left off the boulevard and slowed her pace. Several feet from her rental car, she tapped the remote, and her lights flashed once.

As her boot heels clicked on the sidewalk, the sound of heavy breathing rushed at her from behind. She made a half turn before a dark shadow loomed over her.

A sharp pain lanced the back of her head, and she dropped to the ground as darkness descended like a curtain.

Chapter Four

Billy glanced up from his computer at the station and narrowed his eyes at Rocky as he careened through the detective squad room, waving a sheaf of papers. The papers landed on the corner of Billy's desk, and he clicked away from the database he'd been scrolling through for the past hour.

"I think I nailed down those statements from Chuckie Lo's homies. They're not going down for a murder he committed." Rocky tugged on his earlobe. "Now, if we can just keep them alive."

Billy eyed Detective Denver Holt before grabbing the stack of papers and shuffling through them. Holt, whom Billy had dubbed Rocky in reference to his ridiculous first name, had joined Robbery-Homicide full time fairly recently. The lieutenant had directed Holt to help Billy while Jake and Kyra frolicked around the UK, and he'd been a tremendous asset already with this Hmong gang murder.

"Good job, Rocky. I'll review what you have before sending it to the DA." He tossed the papers into his inbox and settled his hand on the mouse, waiting for Rocky to leave.

Rocky's gaze darted to his offering in Billy's inbox and then back to Billy's face. "Uh, end of the day?"

"Absolutely, end of the day." *As soon as I finish my personal business on an LAPD computer on LAPD time.*

"Sounds good. I'm also running down the watch stolen from that tourist."

"You're the man. Keep me posted." Billy raised his eyebrows as if asking what else.

Rocky got the hint and spun around, heading for his own desk.

Billy clicked back onto the database and resumed his fruitless search for a Molly Jones. The card and realty company had checked out, but searching for a Jones posed significant challenges. He hadn't had any more luck searching for a young African American woman with the first name of Bri. Both of those women had chosen wisely if they intended subterfuge—and he had no doubt they did.

Lawrence Coleman from Vegas, on the other hand, presented a cornucopia of information. The guy had a rap sheet a mile long. If Sabrina were hiding out from Coleman, Billy could understand why. Coleman operated on the fringe of Vegas organized crime—bad dudes involved in bad business. Billy massaged the back of his stiff neck.

He just couldn't picture his sister hanging with criminals. Before her disappearance, Pepperdine University had accepted her into its undergraduate program, where she planned to major in business. Sabrina played the violin badly, despite hours of practice, and she once ratted out her friend to her mother for smoking weed at a party. That image of his sister did not mesh with the loser with the hard stare and messy dreads on his computer monitor.

What would Sabrina be doing with a guy like that? Billy couldn't believe his sister would leave her home and family for Lawrence Coleman unless he tricked her in some way.

He'd warned Sabrina about her too-trusting nature, but she'd accused him of always looking at the bad because of his job. He couldn't argue with that, but civilians had to strike a happy medium between naivete and constant wariness.

Billy toyed with his pen, weaving it between his fingers. Vegas made sense. Ever since Bri had mentioned Sin City, it had struck a chord with him. One of the private investigators he'd hired, Dina Ferrari, had a lead in Vegas, but forces conspired to shut her down when she went out there to investigate. Every avenue she followed had led to a dead end—almost as if someone had been keeping one step ahead of her.

If Lawrence were in bed with organized crime, it could've been that force that waylaid Dina and made sure she'd come up empty. The mob still held power in Vegas and might want to protect even a low-level grunt like Lawrence.

Bri had given him a starting point, and because of Dina's lead in Vegas, Billy had a ray of hope that this location might prove fruitful in finding Sabrina. If not, it could prove fruitful in giving him the opportunity to confront the man who'd abused his sister.

And he couldn't wait for that. He cracked his knuckles.

MIA SLAPPED AT Zach's sweaty hand pinching her upper arm. "Would you stop hovering? I have no idea why Tucker sent you to pick me up at the hospital. I could've checked out and gotten back to my car on my own. I'm fine."

"You got cracked on the back of the head, you have a lump the size of a walnut on your skull and you lost consciousness." He snatched her keycard from her fingers and squeezed past her to open the door of her hotel room, almost knocking her over in the process.

She grabbed the doorjamb, suddenly dizzy. "You're not helping, Zach."

"Sorry." He shoved his glasses up his nose with his middle finger as his cheeks sported two red flags. "Do you want anything? Water? Room service?"

"A stiff drink?"

He wrinkled his otherwise smooth brow, and his glasses slid down again. "I don't think that was one of the nurse's recommendations."

"It should've been." She grabbed a bottle of water from the credenza and chugged half of it. "You know what I'm most upset about?"

"That you didn't get a look at the guy who attacked you?"

"Oh, no. I'm sure that smarmy-looking man with Brianna is the one who whacked me on the back of the head." She screwed the lid back on the water bottle. "I'm pissed off that he took my purse. I loved that purse."

Zach, one of the newer members on their team whom Tucker had sent to babysit her, widened his eyes. "Are you kidding? You're kidding, right?"

"Sort of. It's a good thing I left my phone in the car and had my Molly Jones ID on me. At least he can't make me as a US marshal. For all he knows, I'm still just some nosy woman who was getting too close to Brianna, showing too much interest. They can't be too careful. That's why he made it look like a mugging."

Zach scratched his beardless chin. "It could've been a mugging. That's not the safest area."

"C'mon, Zach. Use your critical thinking skills." She held up her hand and ticked off her fingers. "Woman drops in on Billy Crouch. Woman leaves Billy to meet up with some scumbag in a bar. Scumbag gives me the hard stare and disappears to the gents. I leave the bar and someone smacks the back of my head."

"So, he wanted to find out who you were and make sure he warned you off Brianna, in case you were a PI or something."

"That's what I figured. Except—" she fished her phone from the pocket of her jacket and waved it at Zach "—neither of them knows I put a tracker on Brianna's car before I went into that bar."

"Lucky break." Zach ducked to the mini fridge and turned around with a can of soda in his hand.

"Luck had nothing to do with it. Skilled planning."

She leveled a finger at the drink in his hand just as he cracked the tab. "Put that back. Do you think the USMS is made out of money? You could buy a six pack for the price of that one can."

"Oops." He eyed the can before taking a sip. "Don't put it on your expense report, and I'll reimburse you."

"It's on me for the ride." She flicked her fingers at the door. "You can leave now."

"Tucker said I should stick around at least until this evening." He waved his soda in the air. "Don't mind me. I'll sit on your balcony and take in the view of the boats. Sure beats Ohio."

"Knock yourself out, Zach. I'm going to charge my phone, see where Brianna's been…and check up on Billy. Haven't been able to tail him today." She reached across the bed for her charger on the nightstand.

"How are you going to tail him from your hotel room?" Zach slid open the door to the balcony, and a salty breeze wafted into the room.

"We put some trackers on his credit cards and are monitoring his social media. If his sister contacts him, we have to know about it."

Zach's eyes bugged out. "Wow, he's not a criminal."

"No, but we have a witness to protect. The surveillance is justified." She plugged in her phone and watched the icon with impatience for a few seconds before grabbing the hotel phone and sliding a plastic menu toward her. "You want something to eat?"

Zach poked his head back into the room, his face hopeful. "Burger, fries? Whatever you're having."

"I don't eat red meat, but I'll get you a burger."

She trailed her finger down the menu and then dialed room service and placed an order for Zach's burger and fries and a chicken Caesar salad for herself.

She cupped her charging phone in her hand and navigated to the GPS tracker on Brianna's car. She zeroed in on a stationary location in Santa Monica. Did Brianna live there? Have family there? She could also bring up Brianna's location history to see if she stopped anywhere along the way last night after leaving the bar and to trace her movements today.

Holding her breath, she flicked over to her surveillance of Billy. When she got to his credit card purchases, she swore.

Zach had left the sliding door open and slid his feet from the railing on the balcony, planting them on the deck with a thud. He twisted his head around. "What's wrong?"

"Detective Billy Crouch is on the move."

"He's a detective with LAPD. That makes sense."

"No. He's *really* on the move." She glanced at the time on her phone. "I have just enough time to eat that salad, pack a bag and head to the airport."

"Airport? You're leaving LA?"

"Where he goes, I go." She slid off the bed. "I need to shower and change. Listen for room service, and don't touch my salad."

Zach wrinkled his nose. "Sh-should I go with you?"

"Absolutely not. I'm fine. I'll let Tucker know I'm officially relieving you of your duty."

"Where's Crouch going? Where are *you* going?"

She winked at him. "Vegas, baby."

BILLY STOWED HIS bag in the overhead compartment and reached over to help a woman hoist hers next to his. She smiled her thanks, and Billy dropped into the aisle seat, his long legs crammed into the small space. Thank God he only had to endure this agony for a quick forty-minute hop.

Billy tipped his head back and closed his eyes as the plane rumbled to life. Rocky had been a lifesaver when Billy told him he had to leave town. Lieutenant Figueroa had been less understanding, reluctant to lose both members of Robbery-Homicide's dynamic duo, but several members of the squad had stepped up recently, taking on high-profile murder cases and solving them with finesse. Fig had to learn to lean on some of these up-and-comers, and now was as good a time as any.

He opened one eye and saw the blue expanse of the Pacific through the window as the aircraft made a right turn over the water. He'd been able to get Coleman's home address in Vegas, and he also had a good idea where he'd be hanging out. He preferred to confront the guy in public. He told himself he just needed confirmation that Sabrina had been with him, that she was still alive. Coleman probably wouldn't admit to abusing her, but if he could reassure Billy that his sister wasn't dead, he might just kiss the man instead of punching him out.

Could he trust Bri? She'd been dodgy, but what rea-son would she have to seek him out and tell him about Sabrina? People inserted themselves into cases all the time. He'd seen and experienced it firsthand. But his sister's disappearance was no Copycat Killer case. This cold case could hardly satisfy an attention seeker.

Didn't mean Bri was legit. And what about Molly Jones? How did she fit into all this? It couldn't be a coincidence that the sexy brunette had appeared in his life just when Bri did, telling stories about Sabrina. They could be totally unrelated, but he made a living dismissing coincidence.

The short flight gave him just enough time to down a beer, and he tossed the can in the plastic waste bag the flight attendant dangled from his fingertips just as the lights of Vegas spread below them.

Twenty minutes later, the *ca-ching*, *ca-ching* of slot machines cascaded around him as he strode through the airport, his lone bag rolling at his side. He'd booked a room at the Venetian. He'd always had good luck there. He hoped this trip would keep the streak going.

He caught a taxi to the hotel and checked in at the front desk. As he rolled his suitcase through the casino to the elevator, he dug into his pocket for a few quarters. He fed them into a slot machine that sported gondolas and other items Vegas had decided belonged in Venice. His eye twitched as three gondolas and a double black bar lined up for him. The machine racked up $150, and he punched the button to print his receipt.

With a spring in his step, he cruised to the elevator. He had a good feeling about his trip.

He'd left LA in such a hurry he hadn't had time to change out of his suit. He undressed and hung the suit in the closet. Then he stepped into the shower. After brushing his teeth, he put on a pair of dark slacks and a white shirt and slipped into a pair of loafers.

He planned to get something to eat before tracking down Coleman at the downtown casino where he and his crew held court. He pulled his leather jacket from his suitcase and shook it out. He took out his gun from where he'd stowed it, unloaded, when he cleared it with TSA. Then he loaded it.

He put on the jacket and shoved the gun in his pocket. He had no intention of using it or even brandishing it. He didn't need that headache in Vegas, but sometimes good intentions went all to hell.

He knew the Venetian had a Delmonico's, and he could use some red meat right about now. On the way to the restaurant, he swung by a cashier and exchanged his receipt for cold, hard cash. The $150 just might cover his dinner at Delmonico's—and that didn't include a dry martini. He needed to have his wits about him when he tracked down Coleman.

By the time Billy finished off his medium-rare steak, creamed spinach and fries, he'd formulated a plan for approaching Coleman if he found him in his regular haunt—the Wild Jack Casino downtown. He'd be friendly at first and then ask him if he knew Sabrina Crouch. He didn't want to scare him right away—that would come later.

He snapped the leather billfold closed on several twenties. As he downed the rest of his water, he jerked his head up at a shadow passing beyond the glass partition on one side of his table for one.

He couldn't shake the feeling he'd had since he left

his hotel room of being followed. His heart tripped over itself as he considered the prospect that Sabrina was watching him. Maybe she felt she couldn't approach him yet. But as a cop, he should be able to make an amateur following him. So far, he'd only had that prickling feeling at the back of his neck—instinct, nothing concrete.

He whipped the napkin from his lap and dropped it next to his plate. He ordered a car on his phone and headed for the hotel exit.

Ten minutes later, as the car pulled away from the curb, he cranked his head over his shoulder. Too hard to tell if he had a tail, as a swarm of headlights clogged the strip heading toward downtown. He settled in the back seat of the car. Did it matter? The most important thing right now was finding Lawrence Coleman at the Wild Jack.

The garish neon of the Strip gave way to the even more garish neon of Downtown Vegas, the flashing lights making his head pound.

When the car pulled up in front of the casino, Billy thanked the driver and stepped onto the sidewalk, immediately getting swept along with the tide of humanity, ducking into casinos, clubs, restaurants, trying their luck at one-armed bandits waving from open doorways.

Massaging his temple with two fingers, Billy darted into Wild Jack and surveyed the scene. The vast space crackled with life. Gamblers surged onto the casino floor, hungry diners followed the path to the buffet and women in sparkly dresses rode the escalator up to the second floor to hit the club. Billy followed the sparkles.

He'd had intel from LVPD that Coleman hung out in the VIP area of that club. Billy planned to join him there.

He tugged on the lapels of his leather jacket, feeling the butt of his gun against the inside of his elbow. He stepped onto the escalator in the wake of a swirl of perfumed bodies.

As he walked down the carpeted hallway to the club, a silence buffeted his ears in contrast to the cacophony downstairs. He knew that would end once he stepped beyond the gold double doors.

He paid the cover charge with the rest of his slot machine winnings and surveyed the club as his eyes adjusted to the dim light. A bass rhythm thumped from the dance floor, reverberating in his chest. His gaze flicked past the bodies bumping and grinding to a short set of steps that led to a roped-off area, which was slightly elevated. He'd have to get closer to figure out if Coleman was among the VIPs.

He threaded his way to the bar and ordered a club soda with lime, done up to look like a gin and tonic. Clutching his glass, he wandered toward the VIP area. He circled it once, spotting his quarry on a plush sofa with several bottles of champagne in front of him, his arm around a young woman who already looked drunk. Knots tightened in his gut.

He edged around one side of the roped-off area, closest to where Coleman sat with his crew, his brain working through the ruse he'd concocted to get close to the youngblood.

As he made a move, someone grabbed his arm above the elbow. He twisted around and staggered back a step when Molly Jones winked at him.

"I wouldn't do that if I were you. Someone sent you on a wild-goose chase."

Chapter Five

Hell no. This wasn't happening.

Gritting his teeth, he had a hard time spitting out the words. "What the hell are you doing here? You crashing this party, or do you now have a real estate license for Vegas?"

The strong grip on his arm turned into a caress. "I'll explain everything, but can we get out of this horrible club? I'll even buy you a real drink."

Still existing in the dream state that had descended on him when Molly grabbed his arm, Billy didn't feel as if he even had a choice. He parked his drink on a cocktail table and allowed Molly to steer him out of the club, his heart mimicking the throbbing dance music.

When they reached the relative quiet of the entryway, she pointed to the ceiling. "There's a bar upstairs, and I'm sure they'll have a very dry martini for you— two olives."

He jerked his arm out of her grasp and halted, his loafers scuffing into the carpet. "Who *are* you?"

"I'll get to that when we hit the bar upstairs."

She started walking in front of him, her swaying hips encased in smooth black leather, enticing him to follow. What choice did he have? They rode up the escalator in silence, a million questions on Billy's lips.

She ushered him into a bar with a much more sedate and subtle quality than either the casino or the club downstairs. Its glass walls overlooked the frantic lights of downtown, further emphasizing its closed-off atmosphere.

Molly claimed a table near the window and waved to the cocktail waitress. When she arrived at their table, Molly said, "He'll have…"

Billy sat up straight. "I'll order my own damn drink."

He then proceeded to order a dirty martini with two olives as Molly tried valiantly to hide her smirk.

"And I'll have a top-shelf margarita, on the rocks, salt all around the rim."

When the waitress left, Molly braced an elbow on the table, cupping her chin with her palm. "I know you have a lot of questions."

"Cut it." He sliced a hand through the air. "Who are you, and what do you know about my sister?"

"You sure you don't want to have that martini in hand first?" She cocked her head at him, and her dark hair slid over one bare shoulder, fluttering against the black lace of her top.

He held up a hand in an attempt to stop her words as much as to stop her magnetic pull on him. "I'm good. Start talking."

She took a deep breath. "My name isn't Molly Jones."

"No kidding. Tell me something I don't already know."

She stuck out her hand. "My name is Mia Romano, and I'm a US marshal."

Billy swallowed, ignoring her hand. If he wanted a clear head, he'd have to stop touching her. "ID. Proof."

She patted her chest, as if she typically kept her badge in her bra. "I don't have it on me. If I'm going to be Molly Jones, Realtor, for the evening, I don't carry it. Too dangerous. You're just gonna have to trust me on this one."

Billy snorted. "What do the US Marshals want with me? Why are you following me? Does this have something to do with Bri? My sister, Sabrina?"

She exhaled Bri's name on a sigh. "Yes, this has everything to do with your sister. She's alive."

The confirmation washed over him like a warm wave, and he squeezed his eyes shut, his nose tingling. He sniffed. He didn't need to cry in front of this woman.

Her warm hand covered his on the table. "I know. The best news for you, what you've been waiting to hear all these years."

He allowed the comfort for a few seconds, relished it. Then he jerked his hand away and grabbed the cocktail napkin the waitress had thrown down when she took their order. He pressed it against his eyes.

"Where is she, and why are you involved?"

"This is the hard part." Molly—Mia glanced up at the waitress, bearing their drinks on a tray.

As she placed them on the table, Billy drew out a credit card. "Keep 'em coming."

Mia stuck out the tip of her tongue and licked the salt from the edge of her glass. "Your sister witnessed the murder of a gangster here in Vegas."

The news punched Billy in the gut, but with a steady hand, he pinched the toothpick between his fingers and pulled off one olive with his teeth. Then he took a sip of his drink, the alcohol thudding against his chest. "Are you telling me you have her in witness protection?"

"*Had* her in witness protection. She…left."

"You just let her leave?" He skimmed his fingers through his short Afro. "H-how long was she in witness protection?"

Mia lifted her drink and met his eyes over the rim. "Five years."

Billy covered his eyes with one hand. That was about as long as she'd been gone. She never did mean to run away and keep her family in the dark. She'd wanted to come home.

"I know it's a shock, Billy. She always worried about all of you, but we explained that the Carluccis knew all about her family. She stayed silent to protect you."

Billy licked his lips, his throat suddenly parched. "The Carlucci family? You're telling me my sister was involved with the Carlucci family? Or was it wrong place, wrong time? That's it, right? She was just in the wrong place when she witnessed this murder?"

"A little of both. She knew the younger brother, Nick Carlucci. Came out to Vegas to see him."

"What?" Billy shook his head. "No. She didn't know

anyone in Vegas. She never came out here. She and her friends would go to Palm Springs and Cancún with frat boys and suburban rappers. She never went to Vegas. Wasn't her scene."

Mia stroked the stem of her glass. "She met Nick online."

Billy groaned and took a gulp of his martini, the bitter kick of the gin burning the back of his throat. "I warned her about those online dating sites."

"There's more, Billy." Mia tapped one short fingernail against her glass, dislodging grains of salt. "This was a dating site for, you know…finding a sugar daddy."

Billy's mouth dropped open. "Sabrina?"

"She had a friend in LA showing up with expensive bags and shoes and taking some high-end vacations. Young people do stupid things." She signaled to the waitress and pointed to their drinks. "Two more of these, please."

"But that's like prostitution." Billy savagely stabbed the lone olive floating in the dregs of his martini.

Mia lifted her shoulders. "It's like an…arrangement. These arrangements can include sex or just companionship. Sometimes it's for nonsexual escorts. If it's any consolation, Sabrina never imagined actually having sex with Nick on this trip. She really liked him, wanted to meet him."

He skewered the olive again. "You actually met my sister? Spoke to her?"

"Of course I did." Mia folded her hands on the table. "Lovely girl—little naive."

"Little?" Billy clasped the back of his neck. "She thought she could hook up with some gangster on a sugar daddy website and expected him to buy her shoes for a *conversation*?"

"Something like that, but she didn't know about Nick's family connections. She thought he was an attractive, slightly older man who had money to burn. He is a good-looking guy and just about thirty years old, so not some old creepy perv."

"Just a young creepy killer." Billy whacked the table with his palm. "Where is he now? Who did he kill? He obviously knew Sabrina witnessed everything."

"Slow down. You want five years in a minute?"

The waitress saved him from answering that question in the affirmative by placing a fresh martini in front of him.

"Why hasn't she been able to testify against Nick yet? This murder happened almost five years ago. What's the holdup?"

"The holdup is that Nick disappeared before the LVPD could arrest him. There was some screwup between them and the FBI."

"Imagine that." Billy shook his head. "We've had plenty of those ourselves. When my partner and I were investigating a serial killer, what motivated us almost as much as anything else to solve the cases was the fervent wish to keep the FBI out of our hair."

"So, you can understand why Chanel… Sabrina is still in danger. If Nick finds her, he could…stop her from testifying against him."

"By killing her." Billy's eye twitched and he rubbed it.

"Yeah, funny thing about that." Mia gathered her dark hair in one hand, twisting it into a knot. "Nick was obsessed with your sister. He had a chance to silence her after the murder, but he didn't take it. His family wasn't happy he'd let her go."

"Yeah, he sounds like a great guy."

"Nick's brother, for sure, wanted to take care of Sabrina, but I think Nick actually believed Sabrina could forget what he'd done and they could ride off into the sunset somewhere and be together."

Billy smacked his forehead. "He couldn't have believed she'd do that. Could he? Tell me she never considered that."

"She didn't." Mia clasped his hand briefly. "The murder horrified her. She played along with Nick for a while, pretending they could be together just so his brother wouldn't immediately come after her. But she saw the writing on the wall and understood she needed a new identity to protect herself."

"All this time." Billy swirled his drink, watching the candlelight reflect off the liquid in his glass. "All this wondering and worrying. I thought she was dead."

"I know. I'm sorry. It's so hard for the families." Mia adjusted her off-the-shoulder blouse. "You understand why we need her back, right? She needs to resume her life as Chanel."

"I do, but WITSEC isn't prison. She can sign out anytime she likes."

"Of course. She didn't sign out, though. She just

ran. We don't know for sure where she went, but I'm betting on LA. I'm betting on you."

He waved his hand in the air. "You're in the right place for betting. Tell me about Lawrence Coleman."

She shrugged and her blouse slipped again. "Small-time drug dealer who got on the radar of the Carluccis. They use him. He's a Carlucci soldier. If you had approached him downstairs, that would've gotten back to Nick's brother." She touched the tip of her tongue to the rim of her glass. "You could say I saved you."

"Thanks." He hunched over his glass. "But who's Bri, and why did she direct me to Coleman?"

"That I can't tell you. I, um, ran into her last night. Her name is Brianna Sparks, has a Nevada driver's license. She's watching you. I'm guessing she's looking for Sabrina. She must work for the Carluccis." She held up her hands. "Don't ask me how the Carluccis know she's on the run, but they're tracking her down just as surely as we are. We have to find her first."

Billy scratched his chin. "If I don't attempt to contact Coleman, Bri is going to find out. If she finds out, she's going to know I suspect her. I want her to think I trust her."

"You're going to play that game?"

"I *have* to play that game. She doesn't know you're onto her, does she?"

He shook his head at the waitress as she approached their table and asked Mia, "Do you want another margarita?"

"I'm good." When the waitress left, Mia answered

his previous question. "She might know we're onto her."

She then went on to explain how she'd been watching him, had followed Bri to a bar in Venice and then got knocked out steps from her car.

Throughout her narration, Billy got stuck on the part where she'd been tailing him.

"Wait. You were following me? That's how you got to the wedding? The Chinese restaurant? Here?"

"I already knew you'd be at your partner's wedding—no following needed. I did follow you to that restaurant."

He cocked his head. "How'd you get your order in before mine?"

In the low light, he discerned a pink flush staining her cheeks.

"Oh, hell no." He jabbed his stir stick in her direction. "You took someone else's order."

"I had to give you the impression that I was already there and our encounter was some sort of cosmic fate." She flicked her fingers. "I'm sure he got his food replaced."

"Cosmic fate, huh?" He *had* felt that way. As if she'd been placed in his path twice for a reason.

He watched the slow smile curve her full lips as she batted those long lashes at him. It could still be fate.

He cleared his throat. "And Vegas? How'd you know about Vegas?"

"Don't get mad." She held up her finger and downed the dregs of her drink. "We have a tracer on your credit cards. I saw that you booked a flight to Vegas and a room at the Venetian. And I couldn't believe it. I mean, the Venetian? I'm a total Caesars Palace girl myself."

The heat that had been building in his blood dissipated, and he cracked a smile. "So, you're old-school."

"Sometimes." She tapped the table as she pushed back her chair. "Are you still picking up the drinks? My employer paid for my airfare and hotel, but they're not going to shell out for our drinks."

"I got it." He signaled to the waitress. "Where are you going in such a hurry?"

"You and I have a date at that god-awful club downstairs to make sure Bri knows you weren't warned off."

MIA SHOT BILLY a glance from the corner of her eye as they rode down the escalator together, him on the step below, which put them at just about the same height. He hadn't reacted when she'd said they had a date. She wished it were a real date.

He looked fine in his black slacks, white shirt and black leather jacket, even though she knew he kept the jacket on to carry his weapon. She would've been content to sit in that bar upstairs all night with him, but they had a job to do.

She'd been happy to confirm for him that his sister was still alive—even though Sabrina was in trouble. The news had made him emotional, and she could understand why Chanel—Sabrina—wanted to get back to her brother. But he couldn't protect her from the Carluccis. The US Marshals had been doing a damned good job of that for the past five years. Billy's interference with his PIs and investigations had made it back to Sabrina and had caused that protection to come to a screeching halt.

When they reached the door of the club, Billy grasped the gold handle and turned. "This guy, Coleman, he doesn't know who you are, does he?"

"We keep a low profile in WITSEC." She shimmied her shoulders and tugged at her lacy black top. "Do I look like a US marshal?"

Billy visibly swallowed, his gaze dipping to her décolletage, as planned. "You look like a woman out on the town in Vegas—and way too classy for this place."

He swung open the door for her, and she squeezed past him, a smile playing around her lips at the compliment. She knew this attraction didn't run just one way. If so, he never would've given her the time of day at the Chinese restaurant. His logical senses were telling him her appearance there was some kind of setup, but his emotional senses were telling him it was karma.

As they walked to the bar, he bent his head and whispered in her ear, "As planned."

Mia glanced at the roped-off VIP area, where a young man with dreads and a wild multicolored jacket sat on a red velvet sofa holding court. A bevy of beauties hemmed him in, and a menacing bouncer stood guard.

Billy ordered two beers, the same kind Lawrence was drinking, and a glass of wine for Mia. Drinks in hand, they jostled their way to the VIP area. Using his long legs, Billy stepped over the velvet rope and unhooked it for her to join him. When the bouncer grabbed Billy's arm, he shook him off and gestured to Lawrence, watching the commotion with one eye.

"I just wanna buy the young brother a drink. I think we have friends in common."

Lawrence waved his bottle in the air. "I'm almost empty. Let him in."

Mia clung to Billy's arm as he swaggered to the corner couch, looking more like a VIP than Lawrence Coleman ever could.

Billy held out the beer. "Coleman, right?"

Lawrence's gaze flicked from Billy to Mia before he took the bottle from Billy's hand.

"That's right. Do I know you, man?"

"I think we know some of the same people." Billy clinked the neck of his beer against Coleman's.

"And who'd that be?" Coleman took a quick swig from the bottle, the gold chains around his neck clinking with every move.

"Nick."

Coleman choked on his beer. "That guy's long gone. Before my time."

"Really." Billy took a sip of his own beer, his eyes narrowing. "I thought someone said you knew his girl, Sabrina."

"Th-that was a long time ago." Coleman slammed the bottle on the table. "Me and her was just friends. I was just a kid back then. What do you want? Did Vince send you here to test me?"

"I haven't seen either of the brothers in years." Billy shrugged, his leather jacket creaking around his shoulders. "I knew Sabrina and Nick. That's all. Last I heard, they were in Vegas."

"Her and Nick disappeared about the same time... and that's all I know." He raised the beer. "Thanks for the beer, brother."

"Sure, sure."

Billy went in for a handshake, and Coleman bumped his fist as his gaze darted to the bouncer manning the velvet rope.

Mia slid her hand along the lapel of Coleman's jacket. "Cool threads."

That earned her a dirty look from the woman with the cat eyeliner and leopard-print leggings.

Before the bouncer reached them, Billy took her hand and led her from the VIP area. He murmured close to her ear, "He's still watching us. We're going to have to pretend for a few more minutes."

She squeezed his hand. "Let's dance. We didn't get a chance at the wedding."

Tugging on his leather jacket, he said, "I can't remove this. It's gonna be hot out there."

"Just shuffle your feet and dip your shoulders a little. Put Coleman's mind at ease that you didn't come in here looking for him." She crooked her finger, and he followed her onto the floor, alive with gyrating sweaty bodies.

Across from Billy, Mia shimmied and swayed her hips to the beat. Even expending minimum effort, Billy looked sexy as hell out there. He moved closer to the edge of the dance floor, and she followed him.

When the VIP area was no longer visible, Billy gave up the pretense and ducked toward the exit.

When the doors closed on the thumping music, Billy grabbed the lapels of his jacket and fanned himself. "I almost passed out in there."

"Is that what those dance moves were?" She nudged him with her elbow.

He snapped his fingers. "You missed my real moves at the wedding."

"My loss." Mia coughed and released his arm. They didn't have to pretend anymore—not that it didn't feel totally right to be close to Billy, holding his arm.

"Do you think that did the trick?" He jerked his thumb over his shoulder. "If Bri knows Coleman, maybe she'll find out about the stranger asking him about Sabrina and Nick. Then I can keep her around and try to find out what she knows about the Carluccis."

"She's going to be pumping you for info, and you're going to be giving it right back to her." Mia smoothed her hands over the thighs of her leather pants. "Hopefully, word will get back to Bri that you made contact with Coleman, giving her the warm and fuzzies that you believe her."

They stepped off the escalator onto the main casino floor, the chirping, bells and shouts assaulting Mia's ears. She tapped Billy's arm. "Can you hold on a minute? I need to use the ladies' room."

"Go ahead. I already won a jackpot at my hotel. Maybe I'm on a streak here." He pointed to a row of slot machines, flashing four-leaf clovers and pots of gold. "I'll be over here."

"Don't lose all your money." She shook her finger at him before pivoting toward the restrooms.

Maybe if he got lucky, she'd get lucky. It's not like he was a protected witness or even on the case. At least he was on the right side of the law, which would be an upgrade for her.

She turned into the short hallway, her high heels sinking into the carpet. She smiled and nodded at a woman who exited the bathroom and held the door for her.

She squeezed past another woman bending over in front of the vanity to fluff out her hair and grabbed the handle of a stall and pulled open the door.

The hair fluffer left and someone else entered. Water gushed into the sink. Mia tugged up her leather pants, grateful she'd had the foresight to dress up for this assignment.

She unlatched the door and placed her palm against the cool metal to push it open, but someone snatched the door and flung it wide.

A woman barreled into the small space, shoving Mia against the wall of the stall and flashing a gleaming knife.

The woman hissed in her face. "Who the hell are you, and why are you looking for Sabrina?"

Chapter Six

Billy dragged his gaze away from the entrance to the restrooms as he watched the pots of gold line up on the black bar. Damn, he was on a lucky streak. Maybe his good fortune would extend to Mia—not that he advocated mixing business with pleasure, but it was not like he was working this case.

He jerked his attention back to the restrooms, and his heart stuttered as he watched a petite bottle blonde Asian woman round the corner toward the ladies' room, her leopard-print pants painted on her legs. He'd seen her in the VIP area with Coleman.

He punched the button on the machine and snatched his receipt. Tucking it in his pocket, he pushed up from the stool he'd been straddling in front of the slot machine and strode toward the bathrooms.

He charged into the ladies' room and called out, "Mia?"

A sharp breath and some shuffling echoed in the tiled bathroom. He bent over and peeked under the stalls, seeing two sets of legs in the last one—leopard-print and leather.

He shoved his hand in his pocket, curling his fingers around his gun.

Then he heard a grunt and the stall door flew open, banging him in the head. His weapon gripped at his side, he reached out for the shape that charged past him, heels clattering on the floor.

He took a step after her but heard a soft gasp from the toilet. He spun around to see Mia doubled over in the cramped space.

He lunged toward her and grabbed her shoulders. "Are you all right?"

She nodded, her dark hair spilling over her face, her arms folded around her midsection. "Sh-she punched me in the gut. Lost my…"

As he led her out of the stall, two chattering women crowded into the bathroom. They stopped midsentence when they saw Billy and Mia.

"Is she okay?"

"Everything all right?"

Mia straightened up, pushing her hair from her face. "Just a little sick. Too many margaritas."

The tall redhead waved her hand. "Oh, girl. You gotta watch that tequila."

"I'll be fine." Mia pushed at Billy. "Wait outside to give these ladies some privacy. I'm just going to splash some water on my face. I'll be right out."

Billy reluctantly left her at the vanity, the two women clucking over her. He paced the carpet in the hallway until Mia joined him, her face a little pale but her mouth smiling. "I guess we hit a nerve up there."

"Tell me later." He took her arm. "Let's get out of here. He could have other spies."

They stepped onto the sidewalk teeming with people, and Billy wove through them to get to the taxi at the curb. As he settled Mia on the back seat, he said to the driver, "Venetian."

"How'd that slot machine treat you?" Mia glanced at the taxi driver before squeezing Billy's knee.

She didn't have to warn him not to talk in front of the driver. "Not bad. I seem to be on a winning streak here, for a change."

The driver snorted. "That won't last."

"I second that." Mia placed her hand flat against her stomach.

They continued small talk with the taxi driver until he deposited them in front of the Venetian. Billy cupped Mia's elbow and steered her toward the elevator. "Okay to discuss this in my room?"

"Please, as long as you have some water up there."

"Plenty. Do you feel sick?" He punched the elevator button several times. "I should've gotten you something sooner."

"No, better to get away from Wild Jack. That's a stronghold for the Carluccis."

Billy nodded at a couple who joined them in the elevator car. He asked Mia, "Do they know your face?"

"Not at all." She sealed her lips until they reached his floor. When he ushered her into his hotel room, she began talking as if they hadn't had a break.

"They know Sabrina disappeared, out of their reach. They know she went into WITSEC, but they don't know the players. They don't know me…except as someone who was nosing around Lawrence Coleman tonight." She fell across the bed. "I should've had my piece on me, like you."

"You recognized her from the VIP area, right?" Billy tried to ignore Mia splayed across his bed, her hair fanning out around her head, and ducked down to retrieve a bottle of water from the mini fridge. He twisted the cap and handed it to her as she sat up. "I saw her heading for the restrooms and remembered she was at Coleman's side. Too much of a coincidence for her to be in there the same time as you."

"I'm glad you noticed, although I probably could've taken her." She glugged some water from the bottle. "Once I caught my breath."

"Did she say anything to you, or did she go right in for the kill?" Billy spun a chair around from the desk and straddled it, crossing his arms over the back.

"She asked me why I was hanging around Lawrence asking about Sabrina. Do you think Lawrence sent her?"

Billy rubbed his chin. "I think Coleman wanted to put as much distance between himself and us as possible. I doubt he sent that woman after us. If he's a soldier for the Carluccis, they must have him surrounded by their own."

"You're right. I'm sure they know your sister is on the run. Bri wouldn't have been on your doorstep, otherwise."

Mia swished the water in the bottle, and she began to look more normal. The blanched look had disappeared from where it had been lingering beneath the olive tone of her skin, and Billy felt another knot unravel from his gut.

He blinked, as she had asked him a question. "I'm sorry. What?"

"I'm just wondering about Bri's angle in sending you to Lawrence Coleman here in Vegas." She nodded her head in his direction. "And your angle in coming here. What did you hope to achieve by confronting Coleman?"

He lifted one shoulder. "Vengeance. Nobody roughs up my sister and gets away with it."

"Oh, that's why she told you. She had your number." She pointed at him, circling her finger as if to put him in her bull's-eye. "Get you all riled up and send you out on a wild-goose chase."

"But why? What did that buy her?" Billy rubbed the bridge of his nose. "Was she testing me? Like we said before, if I'd never followed through with Coleman, she'd have an idea that I didn't believe or trust her."

"Could've been a test like that. Could be she wanted you out of LA."

Billy smacked his forehead. "Of course. She'd want to be there to intercept Sabrina without me hanging around."

"What I don't know—" Mia scooted to the foot of the bed, dangling her legs over the edge "—is what's Bri's connection to Sabrina? She never came up in our initial investigation of Nick Carlucci, but she has to know Sabrina."

"Why do you think that?" Billy rose from the chair and stuck out his hand. "Do you want me to take that bottle?"

"Sure. I feel like I should drink more, but I think I'm totally sober now."

His fingers brushed hers when he took the bottle from her, and she snatched back her hand as if she'd been burned.

"Static electricity?" He raised an eyebrow as he put the bottle on the credenza. Either that or a strong current of attraction between them. She had to feel it, too, or he'd been buying into his reputation too hard.

"Yeah, little shock there." She dragged her fingertips along the inside of her arm.

"You're sober now? Are you telling me you were drunk before?"

"If I hadn't been two margaritas in, that witch in the bathroom never would've gotten the jump on me."

Billy grinned as he turned to face her. "Do I detect hurt pride?"

"Maybe just a little." She held her thumb and forefinger an inch apart. "I don't want you to think I'm a lightweight, like I don't know how to do my job."

"Do you care what I think about you?" He cocked his head, and his blood thrummed in his veins as he waited for her reply.

"I do." She nodded her head vigorously. "From one professional to another."

"Is that it? We're two professionals? Billy leaned forward off the credenza, the air sizzling between them.

"I…" Mia swept her tongue across her bottom lip

and then clamped her hand on top of her purse on the bed next to her. "My phone's ringing."

THE TENSION BETWEEN them snapped like a tightly drawn wire as Mia scrambled for her phone. This had better be good. She glanced at the display before answering.

"Yeah, Tucker."

"Are you on him?"

Mia's gaze darted toward Billy's crestfallen face. *I wish.* And how did Tucker know anyway. "On who?"

"Whom." He cleared his throat. "Are you looking at your phone?"

"I am now." She put the call on speaker and cupped her cell in her hand. "What am I looking for?"

"You slipped a tracker on Lawrence Coleman and then didn't bother to follow up on it?"

"You did?" Billy pushed off the credenza.

"Who's that?" Tucker asked.

"I'm with Detective Crouch. You're on speakerphone."

"Great. So, I'm assuming Detective Crouch knows who you are and what's going on." Tucker let out a sigh that gushed across the connection.

"I do, but I don't know who the hell you are and why you're keeping information about my sister from me."

"Detective Crouch, I'm US Marshal Tucker Foley, and I'm Mia's boss. She was supposed to stay undercover for the safety of your sister."

Billy rolled his eyes at Mia. "She had to out herself to keep me from making an ass of myself, which is probably what Bri wanted—either that or to put Coleman on notice. But she didn't tell me she'd put a GPS on Coleman."

"See, I'm not a total washout, Tucker." She winked at Billy. "What's this about Coleman? Is he on the move?"

"He left the Wild Jack and looks like he's heading for the Strip."

"Perfect. That's where we are. Do you think he might be meeting with someone to tell them about our encounter with him? Some woman who'd been hanging on his arm earlier followed me to the ladies' room and…uh, wanted to know who I was." She glanced at Billy and drew her finger across her throat. He'd better not get any ideas about telling Tucker some broad had gotten the better of her in a toilet stall.

Tucker made grumbling noises over the phone. "That's just swell. Did you tell *her*, too?"

"I did not, but it makes sense that Coleman might be on his way to get debriefed by the Carluccis. Did Coleman have any contact with Sabrina here in Vegas when she was with Nick Carlucci?"

"I'm sure he did. The Feds never knew about half the potential witnesses in the Mayberry murder."

"Wait a minute." Billy held up his hands. "Mayberry murder? Sabrina witnessed the murder of Ray-May? The ex-cop working for the mob?"

"Only, he wasn't an *ex*-cop, Billy." Mia sniffed and swiped the back of her hand across her nose. "He was still on the force, working undercover—deep undercover—as the Carluccis' security. Someone ratted him out."

"Oh my God." Billy skimmed his hand across the top of his hair. "I can't believe my sister is involved in this."

Mia tapped her phone. "Looks like Coleman is still coming in our direction. We should head down so we can follow him."

Tucker asked, "We? Detective Crouch isn't on this case."

"Yeah, but he's the only one who's strapped between the two of us."

"I don't wanna hear about any shoot-outs on the Strip. See what Coleman's up to and if he's meeting the Carluccis. That's all."

"Got it, boss." She ended the call before Tucker could get out another word.

"He sounds fun." Billy grabbed his jacket. "As I am the only one who has a piece, I'd better bring it."

"He's not bad. He kinda has to grow on you." She put her hands on her hips. "I'm not exactly dressed for surveillance, but even though I'm staying here, too, we don't have time for me to do even a quick change."

Billy's gaze swept from her head to her high-heeled peep-toe shooties, making her tingle in all the right places.

"We're just going to see if he meets with someone, right? We're not going to give chase."

"You never know." Mia hitched her purse across her body, checking her phone. "Coleman got out at Caesars Palace. We'd better hurry."

Billy called up an app car on his phone, and it had arrived by the time they got downstairs. The short ride, less than a half mile, landed them right at the main entrance. Mia kept an eye on her phone as they joined the masses surging into the lobby of the classic casino.

Billy bumped her arm with his elbow. "Tell me we're not following him to another club."

She squinted at the moving dot on her phone. "Can't tell yet."

"When did you have time to put that GPS on him?" He flicked his finger at her phone.

"I dropped it in his pocket. If he'd taken off that dreadful silk jacket at any time, I would've lost him. I was counting on his bad taste to prevail."

"Ooh, you're harsh."

"No need for you to worry." She patted his arm. "Your sartorial splendor is unmatched."

He slid her a glance from his dark brown eyes. "Is that a dig?"

"Absolutely not. I like a man who knows his threads." She glanced at her phone. "Of course, that's what got me in trouble with my fiancé—all glitz, no good."

She grabbed his sleeve. "We're almost on him."

The escalator deposited them on a floor with multiple bars and restaurants.

Billy asked, "Can you tell which one he's in?"

Mia focused in on Coleman's location, enlarging the map with her fingers. "He's in the one at the end. I think that's the high-end Italian one."

"We can't go barging in there. He'll recognize both of us."

"We can practice a little subterfuge."

"I think that's your middle name or something."

"It could be." She put her finger to her lips and crept up to the hostess stand. She crooked the same finger, and the young woman at the lectern pointed at herself.

"Yes, you." Mia poked Billy in the ribs. "Show her your badge. I don't have mine."

He fished his badge from his pocket and had it open by the time the hostess approached them.

Her gaze ping-ponged from the badge to Billy's face to Mia's face. "C-can I help you?"

Mia asked, "What's your name?"

The woman swallowed before she answered. "Bethany."

Mia gave her an encouraging smile. "Bethany, we need your eyes. A man we're following went into the restaurant a little while ago, and we just need to know who he's meeting. Can you do that for us?"

The young woman's eyes sparkled. "Yeah, I can do that. Who's the guy?"

"Young African American man with dreads and a wild-ass silk jacket."

The hostess wriggled in her stilettos. "Oh, I saw him come in, but he's with the party in the private room. I can't go in there because I'm not part of the waitstaff."

Mia exchanged a glance with Billy. "Who has the room booked? Do you know that?"

"Some VIP. It's off the books. Whoever reserved it did so with the manager privately. I can ask one of the busboys who's in the room. The waiter would never go along with the request. He and the manager are like this." She crossed her fingers, her long nails like multicolored talons.

"Young lady—" Billy squared his shoulders "—this is an LAPD investigation. We could make your manager tell us everything, but we'd rather keep it on the hush-hush. If you can get the busboy to report on the occupants of that private room, you'd be doing a great service."

"Of...of course, sir. I work with Jorge all the time. He'll tell me who's in there."

Mia smiled. "Thank you. We'll wait around the corner at the ice cream place."

As they walked away from the restaurant, Mia bumped shoulders with Billy. "Damn, you can turn on the heat when you want to."

"How do you think my partner and I got the best homicide solve rate in the entire LAPD?"

"It wouldn't be because you're so humble, would it?"

"Facts is facts." He pointed at the ice cream shop. "Do you want an ice cream?"

"I never did have dinner tonight. I'll take one of those soft-serve cones, dipped."

He opened the door for her and gestured her in first. "Do you want chocolate or vanilla?"

As she brushed past him, her gaze swept across

his dark skin, and heat scorched her cheeks. Was he playing with her? "Umm, vanilla…but dipped in chocolate."

His eyes widened for a split second, and then he stepped up to the counter and ordered two soft-serve vanilla cones dipped in chocolate. By the time they claimed a small table outside the shop, Mia had recovered her composure.

If Tucker hadn't interrupted their moment in Billy's room, they might be enjoying more than ice cream right now. She cleared her throat and averted her gaze from Billy. She'd better start concentrating on work. She'd already forgotten to check Coleman's location after dropping the tracker on him.

Mia bit into the hard shell, her teeth cracking it. She let the chocolate melt in her mouth and stuck out her tongue to lick the ice cream.

She met Billy's eyes as his mouth turned up at one corner.

"What?" She dabbed her mouth with a napkin.

"That's quite a process you have there."

They both jerked their heads up at the clacking of heels on the tiles. The hostess rounded the corner, her cheeks flushed.

"Oh, there you are." She glanced over her shoulder and rushed up to their table. "My friend got me the info. The guy you're following joined a party of four. Even though the reservation was under the name Carson, Jorge recognized one of the men at the table as

Mr. Carlucci. He comes in a lot. Anyway, the guy with the dreads is leaving. I didn't want you to miss him."

"Thanks, Bethany." Billy slipped her two twenties. "Give one to Jorge and tell him thanks. Now, get back to your post before you're missed."

She crumpled the bills in her hand. "Thanks."

Billy took a huge bite from his cone and then dropped it in the trash. "As fascinated as I am to watch you make your way through that ice cream, we'd better follow Coleman to his next destination."

Mia picked off another piece of shell with her teeth. "You're an amateur. I can walk and eat my ice cream at the same time. Let's give him a little head start so that he doesn't make us."

She lifted her phone from her pocket and tapped the GPS tracker on Coleman. "What do you think Carlucci wanted with him?"

"You're the expert."

Mia gave him a sharp glance. "What do you mean by that?"

Billy looked up from wiping his hands with a napkin, his eyes narrowing. "I mean, you must know about the family because you're protecting Sabrina from them…at least I hope you do."

"Yeah, yeah. I do." She swiped the ice cream with her tongue to shut herself up. Billy knew nothing about her past—and she wanted to keep it that way.

She lifted her shoulders. "Too much of a coincidence that we pay a visit to Coleman and he's called to a meeting with the Carluccis. Coleman must have a spy in his inner circle."

"Wanna bet it's the badass in leopard print who attacked you in the bathroom?"

"You're probably right." She tapped her phone. "Coleman is heading out of the hotel."

Billy nodded discreetly at the hostess as they passed the entrance to the restaurant. By the time they reached the front of the hotel, Coleman had already hopped into a car.

They gave him some breathing room, and then Billy waved down a taxi. Using the tracker on her phone, Mia called out directions to the driver as the car moved downtown.

"Maybe he's going back to the Wild Jack."

The driver asked, "Is that where you're going?"

"Not sure yet." Mia glanced at the red dot on her phone.

"'Cuz we just passed it." The driver jerked his thumb to the side.

"Maybe not." Billy scooted close to her and hovered over her arm.

The faint smell of his woodsy aftershave mingled with the sweet smell of the ice cream. The scent made her mouth water.

When Coleman turned off the main drag, Mia asked the taxi driver to slow down and take the next turn. "There are no casinos or hotels this way, are there?"

"No, there's some residential—mostly apartments and condos."

Billy hit his knuckle against the window. "Is this Starcross Road?"

"Yeah." The driver slowed down to a crawl. "Is this where you wanna be?"

"Mia, I looked up his address before I left, and this is it. He lives on this street somewhere."

"Looks like you're right. He's not in a car any longer." She scooted forward in the back seat. "You can drop us off here."

The driver veered over and read off the amount on the meter. He seemed happy to see the ride end.

Billy paid the man, and they got out of the taxi, stepping gingerly onto the sidewalk. Billy ducked his head and murmured in her ear, "Where to?"

She whispered back, "If he's home, we may be at the end of the line. No more meetings for tonight. His dinner with the Carluccis didn't tell us anything we didn't already know. He's connected to the family, and they want to keep tabs on anyone who might know anything about Sabrina's whereabouts. We may have lost her, but we kept her safe for almost five years. They never found her."

"Maybe we should interview him, find out what the Carluccis had to say."

Mia bit her bottom lip. "If we do that, your cover is blown. It's going to get back to Bri."

"It might be worth it." Billy rubbed his hands together. "Too bad you didn't put a recording device on him as well as that tracker."

She agreed. "Too bad."

"Let's at least get a look at his place, and then we'll walk back to the boulevard. While you were getting attacked in the bathroom, I was winning at the slots, and I never got to cash in my receipt."

She jabbed him in the ribs. "That's comforting."

"Shh." Billy grabbed her arm as he cocked his head. "Listen."

Mia held her breath and detected a faint moan beneath the dull roar of the street behind them. Then someone shouted.

"Hey!"

Billy took off at a quick clip, and Mia followed hot on his heels, tottering on her own. A man stumbled onto the sidewalk in front of them breathing heavily.

Billy put a hand on his shoulder. "What's wrong? Was that you yelling?"

The man's wide, glassy eyes stared at Billy with a vacant look. "H-he… There's a man by the parking garage. Bloody. There's blood. I saw… No, I thought I saw someone."

Mia charged past Billy and spotted a crumpled figure by the stairwell to the garage. She ran toward him and crouched beside his shuddering form, the ends of his dreadlocks dipped in the blood pooling on the cement.

"Billy, it's Coleman. Call 911." She put her face close to his, pressing her hand against his heaving chest. "It's all right, Lawrence. You're gonna be okay. We have an ambulance on the way."

Billy joined her seconds later. "He's still alive?"

"He's still breathing. He has at least one knife wound to the chest." She held up her hand, covered in warm blood.

Billy shrugged out of his jacket, placing it on top of a bush. He stripped off his custom-made white shirt and bunched it into a ball.

As Billy peeled back Coleman's garish jacket and ripped his shirt down the front, the bystander came up behind them.

"Is he gonna be okay?"

"We don't know yet," Mia snapped over her shoulder. "Stay by the sidewalk and flag down the ambulance when it gets here."

When she turned back to Coleman, gasping and gurgling on the ground, Billy had his shirt pressed against his midsection. The blood had already seeped into the layers of the shirt.

Billy swore. "I need a towel. This shirt is not going to do it."

The blare of a siren drew closer, and Mia said, "It won't have to. I think the ambulance is almost here."

She huddled on the ground, her head close to Coleman's. "Who did this, Lawrence? Was it the Carluccis? What did they say to you at dinner?"

His lids fluttered, and he opened one eye. "Th-they want…"

Mia's heart bumped against her chest. "Sabrina? Do you know where Sabrina is?"

His head shifted and he squeezed his eyes closed.

When he opened his mouth again, bubbles of blood formed on his lips.

She dabbed his mouth with the corner of a napkin. "They're looking for Sabrina?"

His flat eyes found hers. "N-no. Nick. They want Nick."

Chapter Seven

As the LVPD detective finished his questions, Billy tossed wet wipes streaked with Coleman's blood into the trash can. He tapped Mia on the shoulder.

She held up her finger at him while she scribbled her name and number on the back of the detective's card. "You'll keep us posted?"

Detective Morse nodded. "Too bad he didn't finger one of the Carluccis as his attacker before he lost consciousness. Just once I'd like to nail one of those bastards, clean and simple."

"There's nothing clean and simple about the Carluccis. The rest of it stays hush-hush, right?" She sealed her lips with the tip of her finger—the one that hadn't been dipped in Coleman's blood. "Keep me posted," she repeated.

"Just as soon as I verify you're really with the US Marshals." He jabbed a stubby finger at Billy. "Him, I believe. At least he carries his ID and badge."

"I'm kind of undercover." Mia wedged a hand on her hip, and Billy caught the detective's appreciative gaze at Mia's outline in those leather pants and off-the-shoulder lacy blouse.

"I got that. I'll let you know if Coleman makes it, but it's not likely. You didn't get anything out of him?"

Mia crossed her arms over her chest, hugging herself as she lied to Morse. "Nope."

"All right, then. Enjoy your trip back to LA." Morse turned his back on them and stalked off to talk to the witness, still shivering with shock.

When Mia turned her full attention to Billy, he felt the heat of her gaze as it swept across his bare chest. "Were you going to say something to Morse?"

"No. I was going to ask you if I got all the blood off me." He spread his arms out to his sides.

She squinted at him as the red and blue lights from the emergency vehicles played across his bare skin. "Looks like it. Too bad about that shirt."

He lifted one eyebrow. "A man's life was at stake."

"I hope he makes it." She blew out a breath. "I'd like to get more info out of him."

"You're all heart." Billy pulled on his jacket over his naked torso and tipped his head toward the sidewalk.

With his head close to hers, he asked, "What do you think Coleman meant about Nick?"

"I'm not sure why the Carluccis would be looking for Nick. We'd always assumed they were hiding him as long as Sabrina was out there and could testify against him if he showed his face."

"But Coleman said the Carluccis were looking for Nick—unless he was confused. The man might've been dying."

"He seemed lucid to me. I mean, I asked him specifically if the Carluccis were looking for Sabrina, which I had assumed. The easy answer would've been yes, but he told me they were looking for Nick." She shrugged. "I'm gonna have to report all this to Tucker when we get back to the Venetian."

"At least there wasn't a shoot-out." He pointed toward the main drag where the lights and sirens of the emergency vehicles had barely made an impression. "I was serious about collecting my winnings from the Wild Jack."

"Like that?" She tugged on the lapels of his jacket as it flapped open over his bare chest.

He buttoned the jacket. "I'm sure this is in style somewhere."

On his advice, Mia waited a half a block away from the casino to order a car from her phone. By the time he joined her, his winnings burning a hole in his pocket, the car had arrived.

When they got to the hotel, Billy pointed at the ceiling. "Do you want to debrief in my room before calling it a night?"

"Absolutely. Questions kept popping up in the car, but I didn't want to talk in front of the driver. You never know who's working for whom in this town."

"I had no idea Ray-May was undercover. That wasn't included in the news of his death. Doesn't seem fair." He steered Mia to the elevator, the sounds of the casino calling to him. He'd never been much of a gambler, but Mia had to be his lucky charm.

"It sure doesn't. When I joke to people about being undercover, I know that changing your identity to get some information or to follow someone is nothing like the real thing. Those people, like Ray Mayberry, who embed are taking real risks with their lives. Have you ever worked undercover?"

"Here and there, but no embedding. Usually, people with families don't do much undercover."

When they entered the elevator, Mia wedged her shoulder against the mirror. "Do you miss not having your boys with you?"

He blinked. Of course she knew about his family. The USMS had probably done a deep dive on his life. What else had she discovered about him? Did she know he'd played the field after he and Sonia had separated? Not a good look, but Mia had been engaged before, and it sounded like it hadn't ended well. He wasn't the only one with a past.

He cleared his throat. "I miss them. They're going to spend some time with me this summer. Do you have kids?"

"Me? No, but I like them. I mean, maybe one day."

She knotted her fingers in front of her, and he dropped the subject. Seemed unfair that she knew so much about him and he didn't know much about her—except that he felt on fire when she was near.

As they got off the elevator on his floor, he asked, "What floor are you on? I just assumed you wanted to do this in my room, but we could just as easily talk in yours."

"Yours is fine. My room's a bit of mess anyway, as I had to hurry to change and catch up with you." She flicked her fingers at him. "Besides, you're the one who lost half his clothing out there."

"It was just a shirt." He swiped the keycard at the door, and the green lights flashed. "Do you want something from room service? Did you really eat an ice cream cone for dinner? You could've joined me at that steak house."

"First of all, I don't eat red meat. Secondly—" she held up another finger "—I didn't know at that point I was going to have to rescue you from punching out Lawrence Coleman."

"Maybe if I had, he wouldn't be in the ICU right now." He unbuttoned his jacket and shrugged out of it. "That makes sense."

"What does?" Her gaze drifted from his chest to his face, and she swallowed.

"Why you left that beef and broccoli at the Chinese place." He flipped open his suitcase in the corner and pulled out a white T-shirt.

"Yeah, well, I didn't know when I decided to collect that guy's food that he'd have beef. The spring rolls were good, though." She winked at him.

He held up the room service menu. "Food?"

"I'm good." She perched on the edge of the desk chair and folded her hands.

Billy reeled in his disappointment. He'd been hoping she'd sprawl across his bed again, but she wanted to get back to business. He threw himself onto a chair. "Okay, we talk to Coleman about Sabrina, and a woman with him decides to follow you to find out why. Coleman meets up with the Carluccis, but not for dinner, and then heads home, where he's knifed."

"Presumably what he told the Carluccis didn't fly, or they didn't like what they heard." She crossed her legs, and the soft buttery leather of her pants made a whispery sound. "Then with what might be his last breath, Coleman tells me the Carluccis are looking for Nick."

"Maybe the Carluccis believed Coleman knew where Nick was hiding out. Hard to believe they don't know, themselves."

"Did they think Coleman would tell the cops about Nick? Is that why they sent someone to kill him?"

Billy tapped his chin. "Why would the Carluccis think the cops were onto Coleman just because we talked to him? You don't think they recognized me, do you? I mean, they must know by now Sabrina's brother is a cop."

"I'm sure they do, and they might've even looked you up, but the Carluccis didn't see you. Coleman probably doesn't know about you. If he gave the Carluccis a description of you, well, there are plenty of tall, good-looking Black guys in Vegas."

The tap on his chin turned into a rub. She thought he was good-looking? "The attack on Coleman doesn't make much sense. None of this does. Why don't the Carluccis know where Nick is? Why do they want to find him now?"

"I'm not sure, Billy. The most important thing is to get our hands on Sabrina. She's not in the clear by any means. I don't know why she fled."

"I do." He pinched the bridge of his nose. "She needs her family."

"I understand that, but she needs to wait until we catch and convict Nick Carlucci of Ray Mayberry's murder. That's the only way she can guarantee her safety."

"Yeah, the FBI's doing such a great job of that." He jumped up from the chair and had to steady it before it tipped over. "It seems as if the Carluccis don't even know where their favorite son is."

"If Coleman survives the attack, we'll have someone out here to interview him."

"Sounds like another job for you guys. The Carluccis are never going to allow him to speak to the FBI or the LVPD."

Mia stretched her arms over her head and yawned. "Probably not. In the meantime, you need to get back to LA in case Sabrina makes contact. You also need to pick up where you left off with Brianna. Maybe the Carluccis are looking for both Sabrina *and* Nick. Bri may just be the clue to both."

Billy slapped a hand to his forehead. "God, you don't think they're together, do you?"

Mia opened her mouth and then snapped it shut. "I hope not. Sabrina seemed like a bright young woman to me. Meeting with Nick would be a very stupid thing to do."

"Not to disparage my own sister, but it doesn't seem that bright to me to be on a sugar daddy website and then actually meet someone in person—in secret. She must've done all this on a burner phone, because there was never any evidence on her real phone that she had an account on that site."

Mia leveled a finger at him. "You are not an impressionable romantic with stars in your eyes."

He braced his shoulders against the window looking out on the Strip. "Who says?"

She snorted. "Nick probably swept her off her feet. He's a handsome young guy, sharp dresser, rich. What girl wouldn't want that?"

"Is that your type?" He folded his arms.

"I already told you I had a weakness for sharp dressers... Cool Breeze."

The ends of his fingers tingled. He wanted to pull her into his arms and kiss her ripe mouth.

She blinked and launched off the chair. "Are you still leaving tomorrow, or are you going to stick around and try your luck some more?"

He'd like to try his luck with her, but she'd just shut him down. "How do you know when I'm leaving Vegas? Oh, wait, you've been spying on me electronically. You probably even know my seat before I do."

"You don't have a seat. You haven't checked in for your flight yet." She clicked her tongue. "Better get on that."

He asked, "Are you on the same flight?"

"I wasn't, but now that the jig is up, I might as well change my flight. That way we can share a car from the airport." She hitched her purse over her shoulder in a clear move to leave.

Words bubbled to his lips—anything to make her

stay longer. "Are you really staying in the marina, or was that a lie?"

"I'm really staying there." She took another few steps toward the door. "Anything to get closer to you—I mean, for the surveillance."

"Of course." He pushed off the window and crossed the room. "Then let's have breakfast tomorrow morning, and we can share a ride to the airport, too."

"Maybe some of your luck will rub off on me." She ducked her head and tucked a strand of dark hair behind her ear.

"Maybe it will."

She moved to the door, and he followed her. He reached past her to open it, and she turned, gripping the doorjamb.

"I… I'm glad you were with me tonight. Thanks for saving me from that leopard-print witch in the bathroom stall."

"And thank you for saving me from blowing my cover with Coleman."

In her high heels, Mia skimmed his shoulder. She tipped her head back to stare into his eyes, her blue ones unfocused and dreamy, as her full lips parted.

He brushed his mouth against hers, tasting the sweetness of her lips.

She swayed toward him and then took a backward step into the hallway. "Good night, Billy."

BILLY'S HOTEL ROOM door snapped closed behind her, and she made it halfway to the elevator before sagging against the wall, her knees weak and trembling.

He wanted her. She wanted him.

She glanced back toward his room. If that door opened one crack, she'd be running down this hallway, shoes be damned. She held her breath, but the door remained firmly closed.

At least someone was keeping his head. But was he? He was the one who kissed her—if that delicious caress from his mouth could be called a kiss. She'd need more of the same to figure it out.

"Miss, are you okay?"

Mia jerked her head up, as she still clung to the wall for dear life. She smiled at the middle-aged couple who'd just come off the elevator, holding hands and looking like a couple of teenagers.

She delivered her standard line. "Just a little too much tequila tonight."

The woman's brow crinkled. "Do you want us to see you back to your room? Maybe you shouldn't go out in your condition."

Mia jerked her thumb at the ceiling. "I am going back to my room. Thanks."

To prove her fitness to carry on, Mia straightened up and marched to the elevator. When she got to her room, she checked the safe for her weapon and then collapsed on the bed to call Tucker and give him the bad news about Lawrence Coleman.

After her call with Tucker, she removed her makeup, washed her face and brushed her teeth. She hunched forward on the vanity, her nose almost touching the mirror.

She didn't need Billy Crouch to complicate this case, her job or her life—but, oh, she wanted him.

The following morning, dressed in a pair of jeans, wedge-heeled sandals and a yellow blouse, Mia threw a sweater over her shoulders against the chill of the hotel's AC.

Billy had insisted on the full Vegas experience and wanted to meet for breakfast at the Venetian's buffet. Even though she was starving from missing dinner the night before, she never could do justice to a buffet. Billy seemed to think that missing the buffet would somehow break his Vegas experience, angering the gambling gods.

She knocked on his hotel door, and he opened it and stepped into the hallway without even inviting her into his room. He'd probably come to his senses and had regretted that kiss.

She didn't.

"Good morning." He waved a hand up and down her body. "You look…fresh."

She eyed his neatly pressed dark jeans, loafers with no socks and light blue untucked Oxford. He made the simplest outfit look like careless elegance.

She raised an eyebrow. "Do you ever dress like a slob?"

"Ask my boys." He rubbed his hands together. "Are you ready for breakfast?"

"I'm starving, but I don't think going to the buffet is going to please the powers that be."

"Of course it will." He cocked his head at her.

"How'd your conversation with Tucker go last night? Did he have any insight to add to our mishmash?"

"He did not. He was as puzzled as we were over Coleman's dying words."

Billy grabbed her arm when they stepped into the elevator. "Coleman's dead?"

"No, no. Sorry. I haven't heard anything from Detective Morse. He's more likely to call you than me. He seemed quite offended last night that I didn't have a card or any ID on me." She patted Billy's side. "Speaking of which, where's your piece?"

"Same place as yours. Locked up in the room safe." He stepped aside, crowding her into the corner as he made room for a couple and their teenage kids. He put his head close to hers, his lips nearly touching her ear. "Why? Are you expecting trouble over breakfast?"

Her gaze darted to the teenagers, arguing over who could eat more, and back to Billy. "The only trouble I'm expecting at the buffet is when I push people out of the way to get to the crab legs."

The two boys stopped arguing for a few seconds to glance at Mia and then resumed.

Billy rolled his eyes. "I don't think they have crab legs for breakfast."

"This is Vegas." She tossed her hair over her shoulder. "They have everything for breakfast."

Several minutes later when they bellied up to the omelet station, Mia tapped a finger on the sneeze guard, protecting the crab meat. "Told you."

When they both settled at their table with a ridiculous amount of food on their plates, Billy aimed his fork at her omelet. "What did you put in there? The kitchen sink?"

"Practically." She nudged the giant blob of egg on her plate with her knife.

A server approached their table with a bottle of champagne and a carafe of orange juice on a tray.

Holding up his hand, Billy said, "Uh, there must be some mistake. We didn't order that."

"Oh, I know." The server set the two flutes on the table and poured a quantity of orange juice into each. "This comes courtesy of a Mr. Vince Carlucci."

Chapter Eight

Mia folded her hands over her stomach. "Any way you look at it, that wasn't good."

"My breakfast was excellent, and I hit another jackpot at the airport before we boarded. I ended on a high note."

She bumped his elbow off the armrest between their two seats. "Yeah, and Vince Carlucci knows who we are."

"We always believed that he knew Coleman had talked to two people last night. It doesn't mean he knows who we are, as in what our jobs are." Billy stretched his long leg into the aisle of the airplane as the flight attendants buckled in for takeoff.

"As you said before, it's almost definite that Vince looked up Sabrina after she witnessed the shooting and discovered that she had a brother who was a cop with the LAPD."

"He obviously knows if he had Bri staking me out in LA. And if Bri is working for him, he also knows she sent me out to Vegas to find Lawrence Coleman. If he thought sending over some mimosas for breakfast was a threat, he's living in a fantasy land." He brushed his knuckle down her arm. "Don't worry about it. It doesn't mean he knows who you are. He could've just believed you were my...friend."

Mia shivered at Billy's touch. She wanted to be more than friends with him, but she didn't want Vince Carlucci anywhere in her orbit. It wouldn't take a man like Carlucci long to figure out who she really was.

She rubbed her arms. "The last thing I need is for anyone in the mob to know who I am. I wouldn't be able to do my job."

"So, do your job. Tell me what I should do next when we get back to LA."

"You said you can't contact Bri, right? She didn't give you her number?"

"That's right. I gave her mine and she said she'd reach out to me."

"Wait for that. She'll want to know how your meeting with Coleman went."

"I'd say it was an abject failure."

"Not exactly. We know he's connected to the Carluccis. We know the Carluccis still have an interest in Sabrina's whereabouts and, more importantly, Nick's whereabouts. If the Carluccis aren't hiding Nick, he's ours to catch."

"And once the Feds get Nick and Sabrina testifies against him, she'll be free." He shook his head. "I can't believe she got involved in this mess. I thought she had a good head on her shoulders."

"Most young people crave excitement. Her friend

had done it without getting into trouble." Mia shrugged. She could understand better than most.

"You mentioned a friend before. Who was it that got her into the lifestyle?" He clenched his fists in his lap.

"Whoa." She covered his large hand with her own. "Nobody said Sabrina was in the sugar baby lifestyle. Nick was her first and only contact on that site. She thought she'd found true love, or at least an exciting getaway for the weekend."

He slipped his hand from hers and flexed his long fingers. "Name?"

"Even if I remembered her name offhand, I don't think it's appropriate for me to give her up to you."

"If I know her, maybe I can get something out of her." He snapped his fingers. "Have you checked with her since Sabrina disappeared?"

"N-no." Mia sucked in her bottom lip. "It's been five years. We figured she'd make a beeline to you."

"She hasn't, has she?" He hunched forward in the small seat, his knees bumping the small, folded tray table. "Sabrina grew up in LA. We had a tight-knit neighborhood, and she'd known some of her friends for years, since kindergarten. If she trusted one of them enough to join her on that stupid website, she might just trust her enough to hide out with her when she found her access to me blocked."

"Maybe." She shot him a quick glance from the side of her eye. "Why would she believe her access to you was blocked?"

"Oh, I don't know. Maybe because of two women

floating in my orbit trying to get to her. Maybe she thinks I'd turn her right over to you."

"Would you?"

He dragged a hand over his face, his usually clean-shaven chin dotted with black stubble. "I honestly don't know. Maybe I could do a better job of protecting her."

Folding her arms over her chest, she said, "We did a pretty good job for almost five years."

"You did a pretty good job of keeping her away from her family. A pretty good job of making us think she was dead. Do you know how many times my heart stopped cold in my chest when I had to investigate the murder of a young African American woman?" He covered his eyes with one hand.

She squeezed his arm. "I'm sorry, Billy."

They sat in silence until the short flight ended, lost in their own thoughts, and then they sailed through LAX and made the trek to the app car pickup area. They ordered a shared ride and kept their lips zipped during the brief trip to the marina.

When the car pulled up to the Ritz-Carlton, Billy's eyes widened. "Really? You're right around the corner."

"How else was I supposed to keep an eye on you? I'll keep you posted, and you do the same." She waved as she dragged her carry-on behind her to the entrance of the hotel.

Once inside, she braced a hand against the textured wall of the lobby and let out a slow breath. That was the best Vegas trip she'd had in a long time—and she hadn't even gotten lucky.

WHEN HE GOT HOME, Billy wheeled his bag into his bedroom and got a bottle of water from the kitchen. He dragged his work laptop from his case and positioned it on the kitchen table. He'd better check in with Holt today on their cases. The guy had proved himself, so Billy wasn't worried about that, but he wanted to talk to Lieutenant Figueroa before he threw any more cases their way.

Billy needed a few days off to take care of this personal business—and he wasn't sure if he meant Sabrina or Mia. The two shouldn't be mixed up, but there was nothing he could do about that now.

Would he be so eager to dive in if it were Mia's boss, Tucker, out here, tracking his every move? Would he be more inclined to let the Marshals handle their business?

He blurted out, "Nope," as he slammed his water bottle on the table. Sabrina was his business. If she broke away from her new identity to come to him, then he owed her a safe harbor.

He drummed his thumbs on the edge of his laptop. It was probably his fault that she fled. He'd hired that PI, Dina Ferrari, to find her. Dina must've gotten too close to the truth for comfort. Dina had been in Vegas, and the Carluccis must've known she was poking around. Thank God she didn't meet the same end as Lawrence Coleman.

When his computer came to life, he entered Coleman's name, *attack* and *Vegas* into the search engine and found a brief account of the crime. No mention of the mob or whether or not Coleman survived.

He pulled out his phone and called Detective Morse, who answered on the second ring. "Morse."

"Detective, it's Detective Crouch, LAPD Homicide. Any word on Coleman's condition?" Billy sucked in a breath and waited as Morse shouted some instruction to someone.

He was breathless when he got back on the line. "The guy still hasn't come to. Doesn't look good for him. But we have an officer stationed at his room at the hospital. We haven't released his condition, so the Carluccis don't know if their hit man was successful in shutting him up."

"Okay, thanks. Keep me updated."

Billy placed the next call without thinking, and his pulse raced when he heard Mia's low, sultry voice. She could make "hello there" sound like an invitation to dark delights.

He cleared his throat. "Hey, I just talked to Morse. Coleman is still out, and LVPD has a guard at his door."

"Thanks for letting me know. I guess Morse hasn't verified my position, because he hasn't told me squat."

"To be fair, I had to call him to get that update."

"Larissa Pacheco."

"What?"

"Do you know that name?"

He shook the bottle, sloshing the water inside. "Larissa, Larissa. Yeah, Rissa. That's a friend of hers from college. I know that name. Pretty sure my PI checked with her."

"Well, then she lied to your PI, or Sabrina was lying to us when she told us that Larissa Pacheco is the one who turned her onto the sugar daddy website."

"We'll see if she lies to me, too." Billy crushed the bottle in his hand, causing water to spill over the top.

"Hold on. You're not going to go charging over to Rissa's place, are you? There's nothing you can get out of her. We already know Sabrina used that site to meet Nick Carlucci. Talking to Rissa is pointless now."

"Unless Sabrina's with her. That's not pointless, is it?" He was already entering Rissa's name on his computer.

"But she's not one of Sabrina's childhood friends, right? You thought maybe Sabrina would hide out with a good friend."

"She's not a childhood friend, but maybe Sabrina wouldn't want to admit to one of her old friends how much she messed things up. It would be easier for her to seek refuge with someone who already knows."

"Stop, Billy."

Mia's sharp tone made him blink.

She continued. "Sabrina didn't mess up. She made a foolish mistake. She trusted the wrong guy. She doesn't have anything to be ashamed of. Maybe that's why your sister hasn't contacted you. She's afraid of your judgmental attitude."

The heat of anger thumped through his veins, and he took a gulp from the distorted bottle. He loosened his tight jaw. "I'd never… I wouldn't blame Sabrina if she'd just come home."

Mia paused and her voice came back softer. "I know that. She loves you. That was clear to me from the beginning. She wanted to go home, to go to you when it first happened, but of course, we couldn't allow that. I know you're angry and you're taking it out on Sabrina's poor decisions. I know you wouldn't blame her if she were standing in front of you right now."

"I wouldn't." He clicked on the address for Larissa Pacheco. "But that doesn't mean I can't blame Rissa."

TWO HOURS LATER, Mia rolled up to the curb in her rental car. Billy slid into the passenger seat. "Thanks for coming with me."

Mia huffed out a breath. "I'm not going to let you browbeat some poor young woman."

"I wouldn't do that." He held out a steady hand. "I'm in complete control of my faculties. They don't call me Cool Breeze for my threads alone."

"For any other case, I believe you. But this one is personal. When things get personal, our emotions take over. Weren't you going to come at Lawrence Coleman with fists blazing?"

Billy rolled his shoulders. "I don't know about that."

"I do." She tapped her phone in the cup holder. "Put her address in my phone or yours and navigate. West LA isn't far from here, right?"

Cupping his own phone in his hand, he said, "Less

than a half hour, no traffic. That's right. You're not from here. Do I detect a slight Jersey girl accent?"

"Only when I get excited." She pulled into traffic on Lincoln. "How do you know Rissa's going to be home?"

"I don't know for sure, but I did a little digging when I searched for her address, and she works a nine-to-five job. Most people go home after work." He glanced at the side mirror. "I hope I don't miss Bri dropping by my place."

"I can keep an eye on her whereabouts."

Billy whistled. "Folks gotta be careful around you. One meeting and you'll drop a GPS on them."

"Don't tell me you don't use this method yourself."

"Not without a warrant." He dragged his sunglasses to the tip of his nose. "Don't you bother with those pesky things?"

"I'll never tell." She put a finger to her lips.

As Mia cruised off the 405 freeway into West LA, she asked, "You're not visiting Rissa as LAPD, are you?"

"I'm visiting her as Sabrina's brother. She's not someone I talked to originally when my sister disappeared. Sabrina had a lot of friends—childhood, school, college, work—I couldn't track down all of them." He brought his phone close to his face. "Next right."

Under Billy's direction, Mia parked on a street lined with older apartment buildings with no lobbies or security gates. "I hope she's home."

"If she's not, we can wait. You have something better to do?"

"Not until Bri goes on the move." She glanced at her own phone. "Wait, who am I in this little drama?"

He cracked open the car door and put one well-shod foot on the curb. "You're my girlfriend."

He slammed the door, and Mia reached into the back seat for her purse, murmuring. "I can do that."

She joined him on the sidewalk, and they approached the building together shoulder to shoulder. "If she's watching, we shouldn't look so much like two cops heading in for an interrogation."

Billy grabbed her hand, threading his fingers through hers.

She could *definitely* do this.

When they reached apartment 106 in the back of the building, Billy knocked. They waited several seconds, and he knocked again.

Mia's shoulders slumped. "Maybe she's someone who doesn't come right home after work."

"Can I help you?" The high, clear voice made Mia jump, and she grabbed Billy's hand again as they both turned toward the young woman clutching her keys in one hand and swinging plastic bags in the other.

Billy cracked a brilliant smile. "Rissa Pacheco?"

"Yeah." She drew out the word as her gaze darted between Billy and Mia.

"I'm Billy Crouch, Sabrina's brother."

The plastic bags dropped from her hand and she covered her mouth. "I… I… You… I'm sorry."

"You don't have anything to be sorry about."

Mia hoped she was the only one who heard the *yet* at the end of that sentence.

"This is my girlfriend, Molly. I just wanted to talk to you about a few things."

Mia waved and smiled, the happiness at Billy referring to her as his girl totally real. "Hi, Rissa. Can we come in?"

"Okay, but you can't stay long." She glanced over her shoulder, her straight blond hair creating a curtain over her face. "My boyfriend is coming home soon."

"Just a few minutes." Billy spread his hands in supplication, his dark eyes taking on a sad puppy dog quality.

Mia squeezed his hand. Man, how could any woman resist that look?

"Sure." Rissa shimmied between them and unlocked her door. "Look, I'm really sorry about Sabrina, but I haven't seen her since…you know. I told that PI—the one with the car name."

"Dina Ferrari." Billy picked up the grocery bags where Rissa had left them and carried them inside.

"Yeah, that's it." Rissa dumped her keys in a basket on the kitchen counter immediately to her right. "Did you send her here?"

"I didn't send her to you in particular. I had her look into Sabrina's disappearance and gave her free rein." Billy put the bags on the counter. "Here okay?"

"Oh, yeah. Thanks." Rissa plunged nervous hands into one of the bags and pulled out an onion and some lettuce. "Mind if we talk while I put these away?"

"Not at all." Billy pulled out a chair from the small kitchen table. "Mind if we sit?"

"Go ahead." Rissa dropped the onion, which rolled to the tip of Mia's shoes.

Mia picked it up and handed it back to her. "You knew Sabrina from community college, right? El Camino?"

"That's right. She was going to transfer to Pepperdine. We had some accounting classes together and hung out once in a while, but I didn't see her before she disappeared."

Billy folded his hands on the table. "Rissa, I know you and Sabrina were both on a website looking for sugar daddies."

Rissa gasped and pressed the onion to her heart.

"I'm not blaming you. I don't know whose harebrained scheme that was, but it doesn't matter. What matters now is Sabrina's whereabouts. Has she contacted you lately?"

"Sh-she's alive?" Rissa's brown eyes popped. "Is she?"

Mia squeezed the young woman's shoulder. "We have it on good authority that she is alive and in the LA area. We thought…you know, since you were the only one who knew the truth of what she'd been doing…she might come to you."

"Oh my God." Rissa sank to the floor, holding on to that onion for dear life, a tear rolling down her cheek. "I'm so relieved. So happy she's okay. I felt guilty for not telling the police about the website, but I couldn't. Sabrina wouldn't have wanted me to."

"Even if it meant finding her?" Mia gave Billy a warning look, noting the hard line of his jaw. He'd been doing so well.

"But I didn't know who her sugar daddy was." Rissa dashed a tear from her cheek. "She wouldn't tell me. I knew she was using a burner phone for the site, so the cops would've never been able to trace him anyway."

"We could've forced the website itself to turn over her communications." Billy put his clenched fists in his lap.

Rissa's head jerked up. "She wasn't on there as Sabrina Crouch. She used an alias. We all did. I don't think you would've found her on the Sugar Connections site."

"All? There were more of you on the website than just you and Sabrina?" Mia hunched forward on her knees, toward Rissa. "So dangerous, Rissa."

"A few of us did it. It was just good fun. We never…we never actually put out for these guys, or at least Sabrina and I had no intention of hooking up with them."

"But Sabrina went off to meet with one of them, and we never saw her again." Billy cupped his chin with his palm.

"Because that was Sabrina. She was a romantic. She actually fell in love with this guy. That much she told me."

"But…" Billy started, but Mia cut him off with a look.

"That doesn't matter now, Rissa." Mia pushed off

the chair and took Rissa's arm, helping her to stand. "We know she's okay. We just want to know if she contacted you. If you know where she is."

"I don't." She shook her head, the ends of her hair whipping back and forth. "I swear, I'd tell you."

Billy asked in a low voice, "Even if Sabrina asked you not to?"

"I've learned my lesson. I don't keep anyone's secrets anymore. I tell my friends up front. No secrets. Don't even ask me." She clapped a hand to her chest at the scraping of the lock at the front door. "That's my boyfriend. Please don't tell him any of this. He doesn't know I was on that stupid website. If Sabrina contacts me, I'll let you know—after I scream and hug her. I promise."

Billy nodded just as a man barreled into the apartment, shouting. "We don't have to cook. The boss ordered pizza in for lunch, and I..."

He stopped short in the kitchen, the large pizza box almost sliding out of his arms. "Oh, hey. What's up?"

Rissa patted her face. "Ben, this is Billy and Molly. Remember I told you about that college friend of mine who went missing? Billy's her brother, and he gave me some great news. It seems she's alive, but they don't know where she is. Maybe an amnesia thing. He wanted to know if I'd seen her or if she'd looked me up."

"Nice to meet you." Ben nodded over the pizza. Then he cocked his head. "If she has amnesia, how's she going to look you up?"

Mia gave Ben a tight smile. A regular genius, this

one. "We're not sure what's going on, but we wanted to reach out to all of her old friends just to let them know."

"That's great. I know Rissa was really broken up over that. Blamed herself for some stupid reason." Ben took a tentative step past Billy and set the pizza box on the table.

"Yeah, that's ridiculous." Billy stood up, and Ben took a half step back.

Even though Billy had a slim frame, he had the height and a commanding presence that could put anyone on edge, especially with that scowl on his face.

Mia hooked her arm with his and placed her fake Realtor business card on top of the pizza box. "Well, we just wanted to let you know. We'll leave you to your pizza."

"Okay, if—" Rissa glanced at her boyfriend "—anything comes up, I'll call."

They left the apartment and remained silent until they hit the sidewalk. Then Billy smacked his palm with his fist. "Of course, she's partly responsible."

"Presumably, Rissa didn't hold a gun to Sabrina's head to make her create an account on Sugar Connections."

"Sugar Connections—makes me wanna vomit." Billy grunted. "I don't mean that part, but she should've told the police about the website when they first questioned her about Sabrina's disappearance."

"She was clearly covering her backside at the time—and now." Mia stabbed the remote for the rental car, and it beeped once. "But I believe her, don't you? I don't think Sabrina has contacted her."

"She lied before. She could be lying now." Billy stepped forward to open the driver-side door for her.

When he joined her in the car, she said, "By the time I see people, they're done lying. Maybe I'm not the best person to judge whether or not Rissa is telling the truth."

"Maybe you don't need to figure it out. Did you drop a GPS in her pocket, too?" He fished his phone out of his pocket.

"No, but maybe I should have." She wheeled away from the curb. "Dinner? We can pick up something at that Chinese place, and I can get what I actually like this time."

She held her breath as he scrolled through messages on his cell. She'd hoped that invitation had sounded casual. In truth, she wasn't ready to call it quits on their pretend relationship yet.

"What?" He raised his eyes from his phone's display. "Dinner?"

"I thought maybe we could debrief over Chinese at your place…if you want. If you have to get up early for work tomorrow, then we can totally talk on the phone later. Or just debrief here in the car."

He held up a hand. "I'm not going to work tomorrow. I put in for a few days off. I can't do this and concentrate on work at the same time."

"Time off when you're partner's out, too?"

"The department owes me. It's good timing, anyway. My temporary partner is going to wrap up our two cases, and I can dip out for a few days before anything else comes our way."

"Did you tell your lieutenant what you were doing with your time off?" She drummed her fingers along the steering wheel.

"No way. Chinese, you said?"

Forty minutes later, they were walking up to the entrance to Billy's condo, bags of food swinging from his fingertips.

As Billy reached for the keypad to unlock the lobby door, Mia turned to him and wrapped one arm around his waist and another around his neck, tilting his head down to meet hers.

Then she kissed him full on the mouth.

As she pressed her lips against his, Billy slid his hand into her hair, cupping the back of her head. As he angled his mouth for a better fit, a woman screamed at them.

"What the hell is going on here? And why did you get Lawrence killed?"

Chapter Nine

Billy jerked back, his lips losing the warm connection with Mia's. He swung around and met the flashing eyes of Bri.

As the fog started to clear from his brain, Mia thrust out her chest, hands on her hips. "And what the hell are you doing back here, girl?"

The fog rolled back in faster than it did on an evening in June in the marina.

"What are you talking about?" Bri flipped back her braids. "Why were you stalking me?"

"I'll tell you why." Mia jabbed her finger in Bri's face. "I'm his possessive ex-girlfriend, and I saw you coming out of his place. Then I saw you meeting up with some other dude in the bar. Was that Lawrence? So, who's playing who?"

Understanding sliced through the haze, and disappointment twisted in his gut. He held up his hand. "Molly, it's not what you think. God, you followed this young woman?"

Mia narrowed her eyes. "She's not that young."

"Okay, let's take this inside." Billy punched in the

code, the plastic bags around his fingers practically cutting off his circulation. He'd like to think Mia really meant that kiss, but he knew it was just quick thinking on her part.

They rode up in the elevator with Mia shooting daggers at Bri with her eyes. She sure could play a role to the hilt. He needed to remember that. He ushered both women into his place and dropped the food on the counter.

"Who is she, Billy?" Mia tossed her hair over her shoulder, giving a good pout.

"Sit down, Bri." He opened his cupboard. "Anyone want some wine?"

Mia said yes, and Bri said no at about the same time.

Bri shrugged. "I'm driving. Can you please just tell me what you did to Lawrence?"

"One fire at a time." Billy took out two wineglasses and grabbed a bottle of white from the fridge. He poured half a glass for Mia. He wanted to save his for when they were alone together.

He handed it to her, and she knocked back a big gulp.

She wiped the back of her hand across her mouth. "I'm waiting."

"Bri is a friend of my sister's."

"Then why is she visiting you instead of your sister?"

"I guess I never told you. One of my sisters has been missing for years. Bri thought my sister might be in LA, and she dropped by to ask me about it." He thumped his chest with his fist. "That's all. You saw her here and followed her? I can't believe you did that."

Mia swirled her wine. "You never told me about any missing sister."

Bri gave an exaggerated sigh. "I see you two are *very* close."

"Did you have someone attack me?" Mia leveled a finger at Bri. "The night I followed you to that bar, someone mugged me."

"Of course not. That's not the safest area." Bri flicked her fingers. "Are we done with this now? I want to know what you did to Lawrence in Vegas."

Billy squeezed Mia's shoulder. "Molly, could I get you to sit down and watch some TV, or maybe get our food ready while I deal with this?"

"Whatever." Mia stalked into the kitchen, clutching her wineglass.

While Mia banged through the cupboards, Billy took a seat across from Bri. "I don't know why you keep talking about Lawrence Coleman. I didn't do anything to him. I spotted him in the VIP lounge of the Wild Jack and approached him. I didn't tell him I was Sabrina's brother. I wanted to play it cool."

"How'd you know Lawrence would be at the Wild Jack?" Bri wound a braid around her finger while darting a glance at the crazy ex-girlfriend still clacking dishes and silverware in the kitchen.

"Give me some credit, Bri. You know I'm a cop." He held up a hand. "But that's all I did—just talked. He didn't have anything to give me. Denied knowing where Sabrina was, and that was the end of it. I wanted to beat it out of him, like he beat my sister, but I didn't think that would be productive, and I have my career to think about. Did something happen to Lawrence?"

"H-he was stabbed." Bri put her hands together as if in prayer.

Mia dropped a dish. "Is this guy dead?"

"No, he's not dead." Bri rubbed her nose. "He's in the hospital, but they won't give me any information about him."

"I didn't have anything to do with that." Billy spread his hands. "Why would someone want to attack him? Must be drug related...or maybe he was beating up someone else's sister. Maybe he deserved it."

"Did he tell you anything else?" She folded her hands on the table, her dark eyes watchful.

Billy had been the one who'd asked Coleman about Nick Carlucci, but Bri didn't have to know that—especially as she couldn't contact Lawrence. He raised his eyes to the ceiling. "He did mention some guy named Nick."

Bri parted her lips, and her leg started bouncing. "Nick?"

"Yeah. I don't know if Lawrence was trying to protect himself or whatever, but he said Sabrina had been with Nick. He'd just assumed they'd taken off together. Do you know Nick?"

She mimicked his tactic and rolled her eyes upward, tapping one long nail on the table. "I don't know any Nick. He was playing you off."

"I guess we don't have to worry anymore. If Sabrina's in LA, she should be able to come out in the open now that Lawrence is laid up."

"I…" Bri licked her lips, crossed and recrossed her legs. "I wouldn't say that."

"Why not?" Billy cocked his head to one side as the noise from the kitchen subsided.

"Well, Lawrence has a lot of homies. He wouldn't look for Sabrina himself. He'd send his crew."

"Would he bother now?" Billy lifted his shoulders. "Seems like Lawrence is out of commission. Why would he want Sabrina back now?"

"I don't know that he wants her back, but he does want to punish her for leaving." She shook her head, and the beads on her braids clacked. "She's not safe— not by a long shot. You'll still let me know if she shows up, right?"

"Of course—a good friend like you?" Billy stood up, rubbing his hands together. "We need to eat and… uh…discuss some things. I'm sorry Molly followed you."

"You don't have to apologize for me." Mia aimed a spoon in Bri's direction. "I still don't trust her."

Bri paused at the front door. "Just don't get too comfortable. Sabrina could still be in danger."

Opening the door for her, Billy said, "If Sabrina finds out about Lawrence being in the hospital, maybe she'll show herself."

Bri headed for the elevator without another word, and Billy closed the door. He joined Mia in the kitchen, put the finishing touches on their plates of food and poured himself a glass of wine.

He held up the bottle. "Do you want another?"

"Yes, please." She shoved her empty glass toward him by the stem. "I need it after that performance."

He tipped the golden liquid into her glass, where it swirled and caught the light. "Was it so difficult to pretend to be my crazy ex-girlfriend?"

"It was." She clinked her glass with his. "Because I'm not crazy."

Billy opened his mouth, thought better of it and snapped it shut. He picked up both plates and put them on the kitchen table. "Napkins? Chopsticks? Or do you want to use that fork you were wielding about in a threatening manner?"

"That was a spoon, and I'm too starved at this point to use chopsticks." She ripped a couple of paper towels from the roll and slapped down a haphazard place setting next to his plate. "Bri's continued insistence that you notify her the minute Sabrina contacts you didn't fly in the face of the news that Lawrence had been stabbed and was lying unconscious in a hospital bed in Vegas. Does she think you're stupid? Why would Sabrina be afraid to come out of hiding with Lawrence in a disabled state?"

"Didn't you hear her?" Billy formed air quotes with his fingers and said, "His homies."

"Yeah, right." Mia jabbed a whole shrimp with her fork. "Lawrence's crew is going to risk going after an LAPD cop's sister in LA while Lawrence is near death in Vegas. I don't think so."

Billy nudged some rice around his plate. "Bri has to know that Lawrence's condition is not going to make any difference to Sabrina, whether Sabrina hears about it or not, because it's not Lawrence she has to fear. So, what was her objective in sending me after Coleman?"

"She didn't send you to him, did she?"

"She strategically told me his name and location and that he'd been abusing my sister. She had to know I'd pay him a visit. That part didn't surprise her, but the attack on Lawrence did. She didn't expect that."

"Maybe she thought Sabrina might make a move to contact you, and with you out of the way in Vegas, the person paying Bri to do all this would be free to make *his* move with you out of the picture." She tapped his plate. "Eat your food."

"The person paying Bri. You mean the Carluccis."

"Their emissary. That bald bastard who hit me over the head the other night. I still haven't been able to ID him. I've searched through the Carlucci family album, and he's not in it."

"Could be using a new guy for the job." Billy shoveled some Szechuan beef into his mouth, the chili hot on his tongue.

"What I don't get is why was Coleman attacked? If the Carluccis sent Bri to do their dirty work and she sent you on a wild-goose chase to Vegas to find Coleman, the Carluccis must've known you'd be out there hitting up Coleman. Why knife him?"

"Maybe they thought he'd told me something. As far as they're concerned, I don't know anything about Sabrina's connection to the Carluccis. They could've figured Coleman clued me in."

"Then why risk sending you out there?" Mia picked up a spring roll with her fingers and bit off the end. "We're missing something, Billy."

He took a sip of his wine, his gaze drifting to her luscious lips and a tiny strand of carrot clinging to the corner of her mouth. When did food on someone's face look so sexy?

"What?" She widened her eyes at him.

"A little bit of carrot—" he tapped the corner of his own mouth "—right there."

"Thanks." She swiped the paper towel across her lips. "Don't you think?"

"Don't I think what?"

"Don't you think we're missing something? Where is your mind? You're not even eating."

His mind was still on that kiss outside his building. For a fraction of a second, he thought Mia had thrown caution and sense to the brisk breeze off the water and decided to make good on this sizzling attraction between them.

He stabbed another piece of beef. "I do think we're missing something. What did Coleman mean when he said the Carluccis are looking for Nick?"

"No clue." She picked up another spring roll and waved it in the air. "You haven't even had one of these."

"Yeah, Bri showing up here kind of ruined my appetite, but I'll have that one."

Mia hunched across the table, the spring roll pinched between her fingers. She held it to his lips. "Here you go."

Billy opened his mouth and devoured half of it, his lips meeting the tips of her fingers.

Mia snatched her fingers back, along with the rest of the spring roll. "That was a big bite."

Billy chewed, the shell crunching between his teeth. Then he dabbed his mouth with the paper napkin. "Weren't you offering?"

"I was." She balled up her paper towel and tossed it on the table next to her plate. Then she pushed back from her chair and circled to his side.

Her low voice purring in his ear, she said, "I am."

He scooted back from the table, ready for anything, and Mia sat in his lap, curling her arms around his neck. He clamped his hands on her hips.

"Is this a good idea?" He knew it wasn't but was hoping she'd convince him otherwise.

She wriggled against his chest. "Hell, no, but it's the only one I have right now."

When she touched her soft lips to his, she convinced him. He closed his eyes and inhaled her scent—sweet from her perfume and spicy from the food she'd just eaten. It suited her to a T.

He slid his hands beneath her shirt, pressing his hands against the warm, smooth skin of her back. He ran his thumb along the pearls of her spine, and she shivered.

Cupping his jaw with her hand, she whispered against his mouth, "I wanted you from the minute I spied you on your balcony through my binoculars. I wanted you before you even knew I existed."

"I did know you existed somewhere. I felt it. I felt

something in my bones, and when I bumped into you at the wedding, I knew I'd been waiting for you." He brushed her dark hair from her face. "I knew I'd see you again."

She slid from his lap and held out her hands to him. "That's because I put a spell on you all those days I had you in my sights."

A thrill raced down his spine. Mia said the most unexpected things. He couldn't wait to get her in bed and discover all her other mysteries.

As he stood up, his phone rang. He made a quick move to grab Mia because he didn't want this moment to end. He didn't want anything to come between them now that they'd decided to damn the torpedoes.

She put a hand against his chest. "You have to at least see who it is. In our line of work, we have to take calls—whether we want to or not."

He held up one finger. "Wait. Don't breathe."

As Mia made a show of puffing out her cheeks, Billy grabbed the intrusive device from the table. Unknown.

He answered. "Yeah."

A woman's panting and sobbing assaulted his ears, and his heart banged against his rib cage. "Sabrina?"

"I-it's Bri. I need…" She cried out.

"What is it, Bri? Where are you?" As he put the phone on speaker, his gaze darted to Mia's face, all the softness replaced by a hard line to her jaw and an intent awareness in her blue eyes.

Bri's voice dropped to a harsh whisper. "Help me.

They found…" A rustling, scratching noise came over the line.

"Bri? Bri? Who found you? Talk to me. Give me a location so I can help."

Mia grabbed his arm as more static fizzed over the connection.

"Bri?" Billy stared at the phone in his hand, willing Bri to come back on the line. Instead, two male voices cut through the static, and Mia put her finger to her lips. The men mumbled something garbled by the poor connection and then faded away into nothing.

Billy kept the line open but muted his side of the call. He turned to Mia, whose face had blanched, her eyes rounded into saucers. "Did you hear that?"

She nodded. "One of them said 'We'll kill her,' and then the other one answered, 'We'll make her talk first, then we'll kill her.'"

Chapter Ten

Billy swore. "Who are these guys? They can't be the Carluccis. Why would they send Bri out here to watch for Sabrina and then hunt her down?"

Mia tapped the phone. "The call dropped off."

"I can try to get her phone traced. We have to help her, no matter what kind of scam she was trying to pull on me."

Mia tugged on the hem of his shirt. "We don't need to trace her phone. If she drove to wherever she was attacked, I can find her. I have that GPS tracker on her car. She never found that, never knew."

"Lifesaver." Billy grabbed her by the shoulders and kissed her forehead—not exactly the type of kiss she'd been gearing up for tonight, but she'd take it.

She retrieved her purse from the couch and plucked her phone from the side pocket. She tapped the display, bringing up the tracking app she had on Bri's car. "She's not far from here. Where is this location along Jefferson Boulevard?"

"That's the La Ballona Wetlands. Why is she parking there at this time of night?

"Let's find out." She yanked her hoodie off the back of her chair and patted her purse. "This time I'm locked and loaded."

He stuffed his own weapon in the pocket of his jacket. "Let's take your rental. I'll navigate."

He stopped at the closet by the front door and took a flashlight from the shelf inside. "We'll need this, too."

Two minutes later, Billy was guiding her south on Lincoln to the wetlands. As they turned right, Mia whistled at the sight of several dilapidated campers and tents. "Is this a homeless encampment?"

"It is." He tipped her phone back and forth. "Bri's car is parked along there somewhere. Make a U-turn when you can."

At this time of night, the street was almost empty of traffic. Mia crossed a double yellow line and slowed down. "Why would she stop here?"

"I don't know. It's not safe." Billy tapped on the window. "Here, here, here."

Mia veered to the right onto the gravel shoulder and pulled behind Bri's car. Her headlights picked up the lopsided tilt of the car. "That's why she pulled over. She has a flat."

"How convenient. Someone must've tampered with her car when it was parked at my place. Then they followed her." He cranked his head over his shoulder. "I don't see another car, though, do you?"

Mia tipped her chin. "Just that mess of vehicles

up ahead. Maybe they parked among the homeless to keep hidden."

"Maybe. Bri was definitely on foot when she called me."

Mia cut the engine. "Why would she even get out of her car here? I'd stay put and call a roadside service or an app car."

"Beats me." He opened his door. "Let's have a look."

Mia locked the car and squinted through the darkness at the tall grass. A pungent, salty, marshy smell tweaked her nostrils. "How do you get in there? *Can* you get in there?"

"Yeah. There are paths, although it's supposed to be closed to the public at night."

Mia jerked her thumb at the encampment of ragtag vehicles. "Nobody told them that."

"C'mon." He took her arm, and their feet crunched against the dirt path. A wooden sign announced the entrance to the nature walk through the wetlands, and Billy flicked on his flashlight.

The dirt path gave way to a wooden walkway, and Mia crept behind Billy as he swung his flashlight back and forth. The light must've disturbed some of the protected night species, as scuttling and fluttering sounds met their approach.

She hooked her finger in his back pocket and whispered, "I don't see any disturbances, do you?"

He shook his head. "Nothing apparent. Maybe once she figured out she was being followed, she veered off the path and went into the wetlands."

"Sounded like she was being chased." Mia pressed a hand to her thumping heart. "God, I hope she got away."

They continued on the wooden walkway, hanging over the edge every five yards or so, listening to the night sounds. Nothing human greeted them.

The path curled through the wetlands, and Billy stopped. "I think Bri dropped or lost her phone when she was on the run. She cut off her conversation with me, and we heard those voices in the background. But it didn't sound like those guys picked up her phone. Maybe they didn't know it was there."

Mia snapped her fingers. "Then you can call her back."

"Exactly." Billy pulled his phone from his pocket and redialed the previous number, putting the phone on speaker.

Mia closed her eyes to listen for the corresponding ring out here in the darkness. Instead, a man picked up the phone, and Mia covered her mouth.

"Hello? Hello?"

Billy asked, "Who is this?"

"It's Pierre, man. Who's this? You the owner of this phone?"

"I'm Billy, Pierre. You have my friend's phone. Do you know where she is?"

"Aw, man. Night crawlers. There's night crawlers out here."

Billy rolled his eyes at Mia. "Where are you, Pierre? I'll pay you if you give the phone back to me. Or I'll buy you another phone."

"I got a phone of my own, Mr. Billy. Don't need no phone."

"Are you out here in the wetlands? Can we meet you?"

"I'm at my pad, Mr. Billy."

"And where's that, Pierre?"

"One-oh-eight, middle of paradise, baby."

Mia put her hand on Billy's arm. "Pierre, this is Mia. We're here in the wetlands. Tell us where you are, and we'll pay you for the phone."

"I seen your lights, Mama Mia. I know you're out there."

"Okay, then we don't want anything from you but the phone. Can you help us out?"

"Old white Airstream with a blue stripe and a ripped awning out front. Near the head of the line. Home sweet home."

"Okay, we'll be…"

Pierre ended the call.

Billy took her hand. "One-oh-eight, middle of paradise, here we come."

On their way to Pierre's home, they walked past several tents and campers, bikes and shopping carts. People's worldly possessions strung out along the road in a makeshift housing development for the lost and addicted. The smell of human despair and desperation overwhelmed the tangy scent of the marsh, and Mia pulled her zipped-up hoodie over her nose and mouth.

When they reached Pierre's abode, he was stationed out front, waiting for them. His scraggly blond hair made him look like a surfer in the wilds. His beard grew in strange tufts on his face, and a dirty sweatshirt hung loosely on his skinny frame.

As they approached, he scratched at his arms and licked his lips. Mia squared her shoulders and murmured to Billy, "Hope he's not tweaking right now."

"Pierre, my man." Billy kept his distance. "You got that phone?"

Pierre smiled, his rotting teeth giving him a jack-o'-lantern appearance. "Mr. Billy and Mama Mia."

Mia waved. "That's us. Do you have the phone? I'll give you twenty bucks for it."

Pierre shoved his hands into the front pocket of his sweatshirt, which had *USC* emblazoned across the front. If he were an alumnus, the Trojans would want that sweatshirt back.

He pulled the phone out and held it up. The beam from Billy's flashlight picked out the cracked screen. "This is it. Radioactive stardust oozing from the cracks."

Billy said, "We'll take our chances. Do we have a deal?"

"Yeah, yeah, man. Forty."

Billy dug in his pocket and withdrew some crumpled bills. He bobbled them in his hand. "I got thirty-four bucks."

"Yeah, yeah, I'll take that, Mr. Billy." Pierre shuffled forward with the phone, and Billy plucked it from his dirt-encrusted fingers and squeezed the bills into Pierre's hand.

Pierre tried to withdraw his hand, but Billy held firm. "Where'd you find the phone, Pierre?"

"The blue butterfly sign. In the dirt."

"Thanks, Pierre." Mia wished she had some of that Chinese food to hand over. "Did you see the woman who dropped it? Or anything else?"

"I saw her run. She ran."

Billy asked, "Was someone chasing her?"

Holding up two unsteady fingers, Pierre said, "Two men."

Mia swallowed. "Did they catch her?"

"She escaped." Pierre waved his hands in the air. "She hid and she escaped."

"Did you see where the two men went?" Billy tapped the phone with the broken screen.

"Looking for her." Pierre flicked one of the bills Billy had just given to him with his finger. "Do you have some crank?"

Billy snatched the money from Pierre. "No, we don't have any crank. I gave that to you to get some food. You need to get off that stuff, Pierre."

A woman poked her head out the door of the camper, her hair in knots, her dark face set in a scowl. "What's going on out here, Pierre? Who are they? You selling?"

"Shouldn't you two be looking for food instead of drugs?" Billy handed the ten back to Pierre, who'd started hopping from one foot to the other.

"Shouldn't you mind your own business?" The woman narrowed her eyes. "You cops?"

Pierre blinked and seemed to shrink into his sweatshirt. "I didn't know, Eulinda."

"Get back in here, Pierre. You're done talking to them." Eulinda widened the door of the camper, and it squealed on rusty hinges.

As Pierre careened toward the door, Mia said, "Thanks, Pierre."

Eulinda slammed the door after him, and Billy shrugged. "It's clear who rules that camper."

"At least we got Bri's phone, and if Pierre's to be believed, she got away from her assailants."

"If we can believe a homeless tweaker." Billy tapped the phone. "Pierre must've gotten to the phone quickly after Bri dropped it and was using it up until the time we called him, because we have to enter a password now to get in."

"Do you want to check out the area by the blue butterfly sign? See if there are any clues there?" She hovered over Billy's arm to look at the phone. "We can try to access that later."

"We have a tech guy at the station who could probably do it." He dropped the phone into his pocket. "Yeah, let's head back to the car that way and have a look where Pierre said he found the phone."

They made their way back to the path through the wetlands, Billy stopping at every information post and lighting it up with his flashlight. About halfway through, they found the signage for the blue butterfly.

Billy scanned the area beyond the handrail and pointed. "Look at that."

Mia crouched to have a closer look. "The grass looks flattened, like someone went off the trail."

Billy ducked beneath the wooden railing and followed a path of broken twigs and scattered leaves. "She definitely took off in this direction."

"Maybe Pierre was right. Maybe she got away."

Billy returned to the wooden walkway, brushing leaves and grass from his jacket. "But she didn't get to her car, or she didn't want to get to it if she thought they were waiting for her there."

"Poor thing. She must've been terrified." Mia crossed her arms, digging her nails into her biceps.

"Why is she running from the Carluccis? Didn't they send her on this errand to watch me to get to Sabrina?"

"Maybe they thought she screwed up by giving you Lawrence Coleman's name." Mia flicked a bug from her arm. "They hit Coleman and then went after her."

"I don't know." Billy took her hood and pulled it over her head. "It's sad when the only person you can trust is a transient tweaker."

"And me." She took his hand. "You can trust me now."

Billy placed his hands on either side of her hooded head and kissed her mouth. "I do trust you."

He might trust her, but it didn't mean he was ready to take her back to his place and into his bed. Bri's call had snapped that spell.

She shoved her hands into her pockets, her fingers tracing the gun. "We need to find Bri and make sure she's okay."

"And to grill her. She needs to start answering some questions. Now that she can't trust the Carluccis, maybe she'll start trusting us."

They walked back to the road, and Mia ducked beneath Bri's disabled car to make sure her tracker was still in place. "If she comes back to her car and goes someplace, I'll know it."

"Keep an eye on that, and I'll try to get into this phone to see if it can offer any clues to her whereabouts. I suppose she won't go back to her place."

"Knowing the reach of the Carluccis, she must be running scared. I doubt she's back at her place, but I can stake it out. I had tracked her car there before. It's a hotel in Santa Monica." She popped the locks on her rental, and Billy opened the door for her.

"The Carluccis probably paid for that hotel room, so she wouldn't be going back there anytime soon."

When Billy slid into the passenger seat, he said, "The hunter becomes the hunted. She should've had the good sense not to get involved with the Carluccis."

"Maybe she didn't have a choice."

He glanced at her out of the corner of his eye. "You mean like they had some kind of leverage over her? Gambling debt?"

"You never know. These mob families are ruthless. They'll use anything against you." She pulled away from the shoulder a little too quickly, and the tires of the car kicked up the gravel.

"I'm sure you've seen a lot of that in your job." His gaze seemed to burn into the side of her face.

"I have." She shrugged. "I'll drop you off, and we

can touch base tomorrow. You'll let me know if Bri contacts you?"

"Of course." He cracked the window and a salty breeze wafted into the car. "And I'll get on this phone."

"Will your tech guy look at it even if you're not officially working?"

"I'm sure he will if I ask nicely."

She snorted. "You're being very humble. I'm sure he'd do just about anything for Cool Breeze."

"The key is not to be too demanding, but he'll do it. We can see who she's been calling, who's been calling her, text messages. If we can't find her, this will be a gold mine."

Mia gripped the steering wheel. "I hope she's okay."

"We found a phone, not a dead body."

"I hope one doesn't turn up." She cruised down his street and pulled along the curb in front of his condo. "Good night, Billy."

He paused for a few seconds and then opened the door. "That probably would've been a mistake—you know, what happened earlier."

"Oh, yeah. Total mistake. Saved by the bell." She smacked her hand on the steering wheel.

"Good night, Mia."

Gritting her teeth, she watched him walk to the entrance, his gait stiff. As she peeled away from the curb, she repeated aloud, "Mistake, mistake, mistake."

BILLY SCRAPED THE food left over on their plates into the sink with such vigor he almost cracked one. He should've asked her back up here. They could've had more wine, more flirtation. They could've recaptured the mood.

He flicked on the garbage disposal and braced his hands against the counter, hunching over the sink. He didn't want her like that—a box to be checked off.

Their union had to be special, organic, blooming from mutual need. They'd been on the verge of something special, but Bri had interrupted it with her call.

A harsh reminder that they had other business besides their own. He and Mia never would've met if his sister hadn't gotten mixed up with criminals. Maybe that fact marked their relationship as doomed.

He finished cleaning the kitchen and dumped some rice and spicy shrimp in a plastic bowl and stuck it in the microwave. He took the food to his bedroom and settled his back against the pillows as he turned on the TV.

Not quite what he had in mind when he anticipated some spiciness in his bed tonight, but at least he wouldn't regret this spice. He fanned his mouth as he bit into a chili—or maybe he would.

BILLY ROLLED TO his side to stop the ringing of his alarm clock. Didn't he have the day off? He hit the button a few times, but the ringing didn't stop.

He opened one eye and tracked to his cell phone on the nightstand, lit up in the darkness and starting its incessant ringing all over again.

He fumbled for it, and a shot of adrenaline had him bolting upright when he saw Mia's name on the display. "What is it? What's wrong? It's three in the morning."

"I think Bri is back at her hotel."

"What?" He threw off the covers as if ready to run out of his place in a pair of black briefs. "Where are you? What are you doing?"

"When I left you, I took an app car to the street where I'd traced Bri's phone before. There's only one hotel on that street, so I knew it had to be hers. I staked it out from a nearby bench."

"Why didn't you tell me you were going to do that?" He skimmed a hand over his head. "I could've helped you."

"It's all right. I took a power nap when we got back from Vegas. I was wired anyway. Listen." She scooped in a breath. "I saw a figure about Bri's size and shape keeping to the shadows. I think she slipped into a side entrance."

"If she did, she's playing a dangerous game. You're not the only one looking for her." Billy planted his feet on the floor and pushed up from the bed. He flung open his closet door. "Do you think you can get her room number?"

"Doubt it. I don't even have my purse with me this time." She cleared her throat. "But LAPD?"

"Say no more. I'm half-dressed already."

"Does that mean you were completely undressed before?"

"Use your imagination." Billy yanked open a dresser drawer and pulled out a pair of black sweats. "Tell me where you are, and I'll meet you there. Don't go wandering around the hotel on your own. The Carluccis must know exactly what room she's in if they're paying for it."

"You'd think so, but why would Bri chance coming back here if they are?"

"She doesn't strike you as someone who takes huge risks?"

Mia agreed and gave him the name of the hotel and the street in Santa Monica.

"Sit tight. I'll be there in fifteen minutes."

In less time than that, Billy pulled his sedan in front of the hotel. No valet attendants were on duty at this time of the morning, but his LAPD car gave him certain parking advantages. He'd learned from the best, as his partner was the king of taking advantage of parking opportunities in the city.

He hopped out of his car and strode toward the glass doors of the hotel, situated on a street across from the ocean and near the Santa Monica Pier. The Carluccis had spared no expense for their spy.

As he walked into the lobby, Mia sprang from an ottoman in the corner. "There is someone at the front desk. You just need to ring the bell if they don't see you approaching on camera."

The hotel clerk obviously did see them approach, or maybe he'd been watching them all along. He met them on the other side of the check-in counter. "Can I help you with something?"

Billy leaned in close to read the clerk's name tag and flipped out his badge. "Scott, I'm Detective Billy Crouch, LAPD Homicide. This is US Marshal Mia

Romano. We need the room number of one of your guests."

Scott squinted at the badge, his nose wrinkling. "Do you have a search warrant?"

Billy snapped shut the wallet containing his badge, causing Scott to flinch. "Did I ask you for the key? We're not interested in searching the room. We need to speak with the occupant. But if you want a big fuss here while we bring in a search team, I can get that warrant."

"No." Scott poised his fingers over a computer keyboard. "What's the guest's name?"

Mia nudged Billy's foot and cleared her throat. "Her name is Brianna Sparks."

Scott's fingers raced across the keyboard as he frowned at the monitor. "We don't have any guest by that name here. Honest."

"I believe you," Billy said. "What about searching for the first name Bri or Brianna? Or the last name Sparks?"

The clicking commenced, but Scott's frown deepened. "Nothing like that."

"How about Carlucci?" Mia spelled the name for Scott and held her breath.

"Nothing. I'm sorry." Scott shrugged his rounded shoulders.

"Maybe you remember seeing her. She came in, not too long ago. She used the side entrance. Can you look at your footage?"

"Yeah, sure." Scott seemed relieved to finally be

able to help them and invited them into the office in back.

They reviewed the footage and saw Bri, her hood up and covering her face, enter via the side door. She entered the stairwell, but Scott indicated that the hotel didn't have surveillance cameras on every floor, just in the elevators.

Mia tapped the monitor. "Do you recognize her? Have you seen her around the hotel in the past several days?"

With his color heightened, Scott said, "I really can't make out who she is or even if that's a woman. I don't recognize her at all. I'm just saying, if she took the stairs instead of the elevator, she might be on the lower floors."

"Okay, I believe you, man." Billy rapped twice on the counter and took Mia's arm. Several feet away from the front desk, he said, "We can't exactly wander up and down the corridors, calling her name. This is a big hotel."

"We could wait here for her." Mia flopped down on one of the couches in the lobby and patted the cushion next to her. "She's going to have to go out at some point. You're off today, right? If one of us dozes off, the other can keep watch. Of course, I don't know how Scott's gonna react to having us camped out in his lobby."

"I think Scott's quite anxious to help out."

"Yeah, after you gave him the stink eye."

"That wasn't even a dirty look." He sank down next to her and stretched out his legs. "I guess this can serve two purposes—we wait for Bri and anyone looking for her."

About three hours of shifting positions, complimentary hotel coffee and trips to the vending machines later, they got lucky. Amid the morning stirrings of the hotel guests, Bri, dressed in the same concealing clothes as last night, burst through the stairwell door and made a beeline to the side entrance.

Billy and Mia glanced at each other as if they couldn't believe their eyes and then jumped up from the couch at the same time. They caught up with her just as the outside door began to swing shut.

Billy caught it and pushed it open, calling out, "Bri. Wait."

She swung around, the hood falling from her head, her eyes wide. "Wh-what are you doing here?"

"It's time for the truth." Billy positioned himself between her and the hotel's parking structure, his arms crossed over his chest. "I know my sister left witness protection and is on the run from the Carluccis. We know the Carluccis hired you to follow me to see if Sabrina made contact. What happened? Did you do something wrong?"

She laughed, doubling over at the waist. Wiping the corner of her eye, she straightened up. "I'm not working for the Carluccis. They tried to kill me last night."

"Wait." Mia sliced a hand through the air. "If you're not working for the Carluccis, who are you working for?"

She sniffed. "I'm working for just one Carlucci—Nick. He wants…"

A whizzing sound buzzed past Billy's ear, and a sharp report echoed from the parking garage. As Billy shouted, a bullet hole appeared between Bri's astonished eyes before she slumped to the ground.

They'd never find out what Nick Carlucci wanted.

Chapter Eleven

When the bullet hit Bri, Mia dropped to the ground. She turned her head to the side and released a soft whimper when she saw Billy, similarly flattened against the pavement.

In a guttural voice, he said, "Roll to your left. There's cover."

"Is she…?" Mia didn't have to finish the question as she scooted past the pool of blood that gushed from the back of Bri's head.

While Billy army-crawled to join her behind the cement block that formed a barrier between them and any further bullets, he shouted into his phone, "Shooter in the parking structure on Ocean and Olympic. Use extreme caution. High-powered sniper rifle. Lockdown Loews Hotel."

As they crouched together shoulder to shoulder, Mia covered her mouth with her hand. "We couldn't protect her. She was right there with us, and we couldn't protect her."

"They must've been able to track her to this hotel

but didn't know her room number any more than we did."

"Because the Carluccis didn't hire her." Mia rested her head against Billy's arm. "Nick hired her to find Sabrina. That's why they were asking Coleman about Nick. They really don't know where he is or what he's doing."

"Neither do we. Why is he trying to find Sabrina? Why not just rely on the family to take care of her?"

"Different goals, maybe."

She didn't have to explain any more than that, because a swarm of first responders descended on the area. A team converged on the parking structure, looking for the shooter, and she and Billy were finally able to peel themselves from the cement and go into the hotel to talk to the Santa Monica PD.

A few hours later, Mia rubbed her eyes and slumped on a couch in the lobby. "I cannot believe how this case is going. Nothing makes sense."

Billy perched beside her, rubbing her thigh with his knuckles. "Are you okay? That bullet could've easily nailed you instead of Bri."

"Or you." She wedged one foot on the table in front of her. "We may have been the second choice if we hadn't hit the ground, but the Carluccis definitely wanted Bri out of the picture. They tried last night and then finished her off this morning. The hit squad had its orders."

"And we're back to square one." Billy jerked his thumb over his shoulder at the restaurant coming to life after the police allowed people out of their rooms. "Breakfast?"

"I'm up for it if you are." She rubbed her chin. "You're looking a little scruffy, Crouch, and you're still in sweats. You actually allow people to see you this way?"

"Certain people in my inner circle." He bounced up from the couch with way too much energy for someone who'd been up most of the night.

"I'm in the inner circle?" She drew a circle on her chest.

"After spending the morning with me on a hotel sofa and dodging bullets—hell yeah. Doesn't get much more real than that." He raised one finger. "Hang on. I'm going to try to score some paper and a pen from the front desk."

"As long as Scott's not still there. He probably never wants to see us in this establishment again."

She narrowed her eyes as she watched him lope to the check-in desk. Scruff definitely looked good on Billy—anything would look good on Billy, including her.

He returned with a boyish smile and a piece of paper clutched in one hand, extending the other. "Got it."

"Little things make you happy." She put her hand in his, and he pulled her up from the couch.

"Surviving a sniper attack should give us both pleasure in the little things." He rolled his shoulders. "Almost feels like a new lease on life."

Tipping her head toward the blank sheet, she asked, "What's the paper for?"

"I forgot to tell you. This is a working breakfast."

She kept her hand in his as he led her to the restaurant. "Do you ever sleep?"

"At least I had a few hours last night after you snuck off on your stakeout." He nodded to the hostess. "Two, please."

As she led them to their table, she turned her head over her shoulder and cupped her mouth. "Were you here for the shooting this morning?"

"We were." Billy pulled out Mia's chair. "Heard the victim was a guest. You ever see her around the hotel?"

She nodded vigorously as she set down the menus. "She had breakfast here a few times."

"You remember her?" Mia raised her eyebrows.

"The police didn't exactly tell us who she was, but—" she shot a quick glance over her shoulder "—word gets around. African American girl, long braids, extremely fly dresser."

The hostess's gaze darted from Mia to Billy, flicking over their rumpled clothing, clearly indicating that neither of them was an extremely fly dresser.

"She ever meet anyone here?" Billy planted his elbows on the table.

"No, cops asked me that already. She was always alone, always on her phone, but then, who isn't?" She shrugged.

When she left and the waiter took their order, Billy smoothed out the paper on the table. He began to scribble as he talked. "Sabrina leaves WITSEC and triggers one search party or two?"

"What do you mean?" Mia dumped some cream into her coffee, licking a droplet from her finger.

"Nick Carlucci, wherever he is, found out and sent Bri and her handler, the bald guy you saw in the bar, to look for her, directing them to LA and me."

"Right." She cocked her head. "That's one search party, and the second is the Carlucci family, minus Nick."

"Do you have any evidence that the family is looking for her, or are they just looking for Nick? Maybe they're hoping Nick leads them to Sabrina, and they can take care of the...problem that way."

"If they're not looking for her—" she clasped his hand briefly "—sorry for this, they should be. She can put Nick away by implicating him in the murder of Ray-May."

"Okay, let's just assume both parties are looking for Sabrina." He dabbed his forehead with a napkin.

Must be hard for him to talk about this case dispassionately when his sister was the target.

"Why are they going about it separately? Why did they just kill Nick's emissary?" He blew on his coffee before taking a sip. "You said something out there when we were taking cover—something about different motives."

"That's right. The Carluccis want to find Sabrina and...stop her from testifying against Nick." She drew some lines in the tablecloth with her spoon handle.

"And Nick? Doesn't he want the same thing? It's his head on the chopping block. He's the one who pulled the trigger, even if it was on the family's orders, which he'll probably never admit."

"Nick may want to stop Sabrina from testifying, but he doesn't want to kill her." Mia stared at the creamy swirls in her coffee cup.

She glanced up as silence engulfed the table. Billy was gazing into his own coffee cup, a crease between his eyebrows.

He put the cup down, and the brown liquid sloshed over the rim. "What do you mean? He wants to kidnap her or something? How long does he expect to hold her captive?"

"Maybe...maybe he still loves her." Mia pressed her lips together and folded her hands in her lap.

"Are you serious?" Billy pushed his cup away, and more coffee spilled on the table.

The waiter appeared with their food. "I'll clean that up for you and top off your coffee, sir."

He glanced at the stain on the tablecloth. "Yeah, sorry about that."

When the waiter left, Mia sawed into her veggie omelet. "What's so unbelievable about that, Billy? They met online, clicked enough that he invited her to Vegas and were enjoying each other's company until the family ordered Nick to take care of Ray-May.

"Enjoying each other's company?" Billy gripped the edge of the table. "D-did Sabrina say that?"

"I'm sorry, but she did." Mia dipped her spoon into the silver container of salsa the waiter had brought for Billy's huevos rancheros and dumped some on her plate.

"Nick Carlucci is a killer. He's a mobster. Sabrina would never fall for someone like that." He huffed out a breath and attacked his eggs as if they were Nick's face.

"She didn't know who or what he was. Nick Carlucci is a very good-looking man—a hottie with a body." Billy leveled a gaze at her, and her cheeks warmed. "As the young ladies would say."

"I cannot wrap my mind around that. Does he actually believe Sabrina would run away with him?" He tipped the salsa container over his plate and then froze. "Wait a minute. Do *you* believe she'd run away with Nick?"

"I'm not saying that. No, I don't believe she would. She watched him shoot a man. Whatever feelings she had for Nick, and she *did* have feelings for him, died in that moment, but—" she waved her fork at Billy "—Nick did have an opportunity to take care of Sabrina right away, and he didn't do it."

"What happened that day?" Billy nodded at the waiter as he filled his coffee cup to the brim. "I was afraid to ask you before."

"According to Sabrina, she was going to surprise Nick at his house with…um…some romantic time in the master bathroom. Nick had sent her out shopping and didn't realize she was there. Big brother Vince Carlucci sends Ray-May to Nick's house to pick up some money, but he's really sending him to meet his maker, as he'd discovered Ray was working undercover. This was Nick's big test to prove his loyalty to the family. Nick didn't handle it with professionalism, and Ray fought back, making a lot of noise. Sabrina heard the commotion and crept downstairs in time to see Nick shoot Ray."

Massaging his temple, Billy said, "I can't believe she was there when this went down. What happened next?"

"Sabrina gave away her presence, and Nick tried to appease her. He could've just shot her." Mia lifted her shoulders. "He didn't, and she left."

"Called the police?"

"Not right away. She hid out, realizing she was in danger, and then she contacted the police on a burner phone. Once the Carluccis knew the Feds had a witness, they vowed to *take care of her* and send Nick into hiding, we think."

"Maybe they did send him into hiding, and he escaped like Sabrina did." Billy covered his mouth with his hand. "Maybe they did plan something together."

"I don't think so, Billy." Mia dug into her omelet again. "Sabrina kept saying she thought she knew Nick, but he was a killer. She wouldn't be able to overlook that, no matter how much she believed herself to be in love with him."

"In love with Nick Carlucci." Billy had heard enough. He spent the next several minutes making up for lost time and shoveling food in his mouth with angry gusto.

Mia finished her own breakfast and then tapped the paper on the table with her fingernail. "Can we agree that Nick used Bri and her associate to look for Sabrina on his own, without his family's knowledge?"

"Until recently. They must've just found out Nick was acting under his own agency to find Sabrina—probably when Bri sent me on that fool's errand to Vegas to talk to Coleman."

She picked up the pen and jotted down the info, putting an X through Bri's name. "Now the Carluccis are looking for Nick and Sabrina."

"And they know his goal, as you called it before, is different from theirs." He pushed his empty plate away, catching a smear of egg yolk on the tip of his finger. "Tell me something. You've worked with these mobsters before. Would they go after one of their own? If they thought a family member would turn state's evidence, would they take him out?"

Mia mumbled, "Or her."

"What?"

"They're ruthless, Billy. It's all about the family, and I don't necessarily mean the blood family. Remember Fredo from *The Godfather*? Did they spare him once he crossed the family?" She drilled her knuckle into the piece of paper.

"So, Nick is Fredo."

"Something like that, unless they can convince him to give up on Sabrina." Mia took a deep breath and met Billy's dark eyes. "They might force Nick to prove his loyalty to the family, like they did with the Ray-May murder, by having him kill Sabrina."

"I don't even want to think about that." Billy twisted his napkin in his hands. "Where is she? Do you think she's here in LA? If she's trying to contact me, she hasn't done a very good job of it yet. I haven't seen one message, one clue that she's here."

"She knows you're being watched, and she's doing a very good job of staying out of sight. We can't find her, Nick can't find her, the Carluccis can't find her."

"That gives me some comfort. If she wanted to be with Nick, she'd arrange for him to find her and they'd go off into the sunset, or whatever he thinks is going to happen." He swirled the dregs of his coffee. "This won't be over for her until the FBI captures Nick and she testifies against him. I mean, she doesn't have anything on the rest of the family, right? She's no threat to the Carluccis."

"She only has knowledge that Nick shot Ray Mayberry. She didn't even know Nick's family was the mob." She swept up the check as soon as the waiter dropped it on their table. "If the FBI arrests Nick and Sabrina testifies against him, that should secure her some peace of mind. Of course, there's another event that could end her WITSEC status."

"What's that?"

"Nick's death." She rapped her knuckles on the table. "I got the check. Let's get out of here, and maybe we can catch a few winks."

Billy pushed back from his chair and ran his tongue along his front teeth. "I need to brush my teeth before I take a shower or hit the sack. Then I…we need to brainstorm ways to get Sabrina to contact me."

"And when she does?" Mia took a deep breath of the sea air as they stepped outside. "What are you going to encourage her to do?"

"Look." Billy pointed at his dark sedan parked in front of the hotel, two Santa Monica PD cars behind it and a news van in front of it. "It's still here."

"You're lucky they didn't tow you. That's why I didn't drive here myself." She tried to catch his eye as he opened the passenger door for her, but he gazed over her head.

When he got behind the wheel, she asked, "Well? What'll you do if or when Sabrina does reach out to you?"

He clasped both hands at the top of his steering wheel. "I know the right answer. I know the answer you want to hear, but I'm not sure I can recommend that she go back into WITSEC, where I'll never see her again."

She ran a finger along his tense forearm, corded with muscle. "You can't protect Sabrina from the Carluccis, Billy, not unless you want to go into hiding yourself. You wouldn't be able to live your life, do your job, see your boys."

"She could come out in the open if the Carluccis were dead or in prison." He started the engine and pulled away from the hotel.

"The Feds are working on that, but we need to keep Sabrina safe to make that happen." She blew out a breath. "I'll help you figure out a way to draw her out. We both want that, and maybe we can start with Bri's associate—the bald guy who hit me over the head. Now that Bri is…gone, Nick will use someone else to continue his search."

"That sounds like a good starting point." He jabbed

a finger at the phone in her hand. "You ever going to answer that?"

"Tucker's been trying to reach me all morning. I suppose I might as well get it over with." Without thinking, she answered the call and put it on speaker. Billy was as much a part of this case as the US Marshals—whether Tucker liked that or not. But she didn't have to throw it in his face.

As she said hello to Tucker, she poked Billy in the arm and put a finger to her lips.

Tucker said, "Finally. Where the hell have you been? I assume you know about the hit on Brianna Sparks."

"I was there when it happened."

"Oh, God." A smacking sound echoed over the line. Mia hoped Tucker hadn't hit his own head. "I had a bad feeling about that. Did you get anything out of her before she died? Or was this another near miss, like Lawrence Coleman?"

Mia clenched her jaw for a second. "I wouldn't call either of those a near miss. Bri is dead and Lawrence is hanging on by a thread."

"You know what I mean, Mia. Don't get holier-than-thou on me, because you're in the wrong. Did you get any valuable information from Bri?"

"I think so, yes."

Tucker snapped back after just a few seconds of silence. "Are you going to tell me, or am I going to have to guess?"

Mia licked her lips. "Bri indicated that she was working for Nick Carlucci, not the Carlucci family.

Nick is trying to find Sabrina outside of the family concern. That would jibe with Coleman's statement that the Carluccis are looking for Nick. They don't know where he is, and that's good news for us. He's on his own. He doesn't have the family's protection."

Billy nodded beside her as he pulled into the traffic on Lincoln.

Tucker whistled through his teeth. "That's interesting. If Nick is searching on his own, he probably doesn't have the same agenda as his brother."

"That's exactly what I'm thinking. He might—" Mia bit her bottom lip "—he might want to convince Sabrina to get back with him, to run away with him."

"We can use that, Mia."

"Use Sabrina as bait?" She threw a side glance at Billy's tight jaw. "That's dangerous, Tucker."

"Sure it is. You should know that more than anyone."

Mia's heart slammed against her chest as she made a grab for her phone in the cup holder. She knocked it to the floor and Tucker's voice continued to fill the car.

"Even before you became a US marshal, you almost single-handedly brought down the Guardino family by exploiting your relationship with the son. History repeats, and you can use your experience to convince Sabrina, just as we discussed."

Chapter Twelve

Billy jerked his head to the side as Mia bent over to retrieve her phone from the floor, her hair creating a dark curtain over her face.

In a muffled voice, she said, "Yeah, I gotta go, Tucker. We'll talk later."

She uncurled her body and stuffed her phone in her pocket, her head turned away from him toward the window.

Billy maneuvered into the parking lot of a fast-food joint and cut the engine. Wiping his palms on the thighs of his sweats, he asked, "Are you gonna tell me what Tucker was talking about? Who are the Guardinos, and what kind of relationship did you have with the son?"

Mia slumped in her seat, clasping her hands between her knees. "It was… It happened so long ago."

"You're what? Thirty?" He raised one eyebrow. "It couldn't have happened that long ago. Oh."

"What?" She twisted her head to the side, her hair slipping away from her pale face."

"You mentioned dating someone on the wrong side of the law before." He rubbed his forehead with his thumb and middle finger. "I figured it was someone who sold weed or maybe a white-collar embezzler. A mobster?"

"I didn't know. Just like Sabrina, I didn't know." She gathered her hair in a ponytail and wrapped it around her hand.

"You must've found out, though, if you informed on him."

"Yeah, I knew...eventually."

"How'd you wind him up? And why?" Billy studied Mia's face as if he'd never seen it before, his exhaustion a thing of the past. "Was it out of civic duty or something more dramatic like Sabrina's situation?"

"It was...sort of coerced." She held up her hands. "Not that I didn't understand it was the right thing to do, but I was scared. I was only nineteen at the time."

"Who coerced you, the Feds?" His fingers itched to sweep a lock of hair from her eyes, but he was afraid if he touched her, she'd break into pieces.

"Of course the Feds." Her lips twisted. "Don't ask me how I ended up working for them. Stockholm syndrome, maybe."

"How'd they coerce you, Mia? What did they have on you? Did this guy make you do something illegal?"

"Oh, nothing like that." She sucked her bottom lip between her teeth, and the skin turned white. "Worse."

A bead of sweat rolled down the side of his face, and Billy cracked open his window. He watched a homeless guy dig through the trash and victoriously pull out a scrunched paper bag that contained the remnants of someone's meal. He waited through the silence, waited for Mia to trust him.

She planted her hands on her knees and exhaled a long breath. "I'm from a mob family, Billy. Romano is my mother's maiden name. My father is Chuckie Petrelli. He's in federal prison for racketeering, fraud and conspiracy to commit murder."

Her words hung in the air between them.

He forced the words from his throat. "Go on."

"Michael Guardino was just someone who worked with my dad in waste management. I had no idea at the time that waste management was a money-laundering cover business for the mob. My dad was a soldier for the Guardinos—not a big shot, not a capo—so he was only too happy to encourage the relationship between me and Michael. Thought it would move him up the family ladder if he could count the Guardinos as in-laws."

"That's—" Billy tugged on his ear "—messed up. Your father didn't think to tell you to keep away from Michael for your own safety?"

"The opposite."

"And your mother?"

"She'd left him a few years before. Took my younger sisters and moved to Florida."

He cocked his head. "She didn't take you?"

"I didn't want to leave. I was in the middle of high school. I loved my dad. I didn't understand why she left him. Nobody mentioned the mob. Maybe if she had, I would've left with her and the girls."

"When did you find out about your father's connections? When did you find out about Michael Guardino?" His fingers had been inching closer to hers, gripping the side of the seat, and now he entwined them with hers.

"When my father was arrested."

He snapped the fingers of his other hand. "That's how the Feds convinced you to entrap Michael?"

"They said they'd go easier on my dad if I cooperated and wore a wire."

Billy's mouth dropped open. "You wore a wire with a mobster?"

She rubbed her eye, which had started twitching at the corner. "A junior mobster. Michael was only twenty-one himself."

"This is the guy you were engaged to?"

She bobbed her head, her chin almost touching her chest. "Young love. We were both attending the local community college, had a couple of classes together."

"Michael never once told you about his family?"

"Nope. His father and mine were in the same business. That's all I knew. He didn't live any more lavishly than anyone else we knew. We were all upper-middle class, but nobody was driving Ferraris or vacationing on their private islands."

"So, you did it."

"I wanted to help Dad, and I felt I deserved to pay that penance for being so stupid."

"You were a kid, Mia." He laced his fingers with hers. "That must've been hard, to betray Michael like that."

Her shoulders rose and fell quickly. "He had betrayed me. He never told me about his family business—*our* family business. He'd already started down the path, so it's not like he wasn't going to follow in his father's footsteps. He surely was."

"You got him to talk, to reveal the Guardinos' secrets."

"That, I did." She disentangled her fingers from his. "They arrested him, his father and many of the Guardinos. My father got a lighter sentence, and I took off for Florida and became a Gator. When I graduated, the Feds approached me about employment, and it seemed like a good fit. If they could forgive my criminal connections, I could forgive them for stripping me of my naivete and dreams."

"That's why—" he pinched the bridge of his nose "—you're so understanding of Sabrina. You see yourself in her."

"Sort of, but she was more innocent than I was. She was not born into the mob. She stumbled into it through no fault of her own." Mia fanned herself with her hand and hit her knuckle against her window. "It's hot in here."

Billy buzzed down her window. "And now you and Tucker expect *her* to do the right thing."

She turned her blue eyes on him. "Wait. What does that mean?"

"Tucker said it. You expect to use her as bait to reel in Nick—just as you discussed."

"That was Tucker. I never agreed to that plan."

"C'mon, Mia. It's what you both expect, isn't it? I could see the wheels turning in your head as soon as you realized Nick wasn't out to kill Sabrina. It worked before with you and Michael. History does repeat." Billy drilled his knuckle against the starter button, and the engine growled to life.

"You're mad?" Mia clicked her seat belt.

Was he? After hearing Mia's story, he felt as if she'd had an ulterior motive all this time—a motive she'd kept hidden from him.

"Not mad." He stepped on the gas as he turned onto the crowded boulevard, and his tires squealed.

"You're...something."

"Confused. Let's call it confused. I don't even know where I'm going. You're still at the hotel?"

"Yeah, same place. Close to your place."

"Of course." His emotions warred in his brain as they drove in silence. His heart ached for the young Mia Petrelli, her hopes dashed, her world upended, forced into a dangerous situation to betray a boy she loved to save a father she loved—neither of whom turned out to be the person she thought he was. But had that experience turned her into a cynic? Did she expect the same kind of sacrifice from his sister? Was she wrong to expect it?

When he pulled in front of her hotel, he reached out and grabbed her hand before she exited the car. "Thank you for telling me about your past, Mia. I'm sorry you went through all of that."

She sniffed. "I want what's best for Sabrina. I really do, but maybe what's best for her is to end the Carluccis so that she can leave Chanel Davis behind and get back to her life as Sabrina Crouch."

She slipped from his grasp and slammed the car door. He watched her disappear through the glass doors before pulling away.

When he stepped into his condo, he felt as if he'd been away for a week. He spotted Bri's phone on his kitchen counter. He'd run out of his place so fast this morning, he'd forgotten to bring it with him.

Now she wouldn't need it.

He placed a call to Brandon Nguyen, their tech whiz at the station. Brandon agreed to meet him at the station to get the phone and start a forensic deep dive on it. Sleep would have to wait, but a shower and a change of clothing couldn't. He had an image to maintain.

An hour later, showered and dressed in a pair of ankle-skimming dark jeans, his favorite low-tops and a plain dark green T-shirt, he set off for the Northwest Division. He didn't want anyone to see him there on what was supposed to be a day off, so he'd arranged to meet Brandon on the sidewalk down the block from the station.

When Billy arrived, Brandon was waiting for him and jogged to his car. He leaned in the passenger window. "I'll get right on this, Cool Breeze."

"Am I missing anything?"

"Naw, actually the place seems quiet without you and McAllister stirring things up."

"I appreciate it, man. Let me know when you find something."

Brandon was already tapping at the phone. "Frequently called numbers? Texts?"

"You got it. Probably everything's going to be burners and untraceable lines, but you know the drill."

"I'll get back to you on my way home from work."

Billy drove off, knowing the phone was in good hands. Brandon should be able to get something from Bri's phone. There had to be a way to track down Nick Carlucci. Then what?

He couldn't go in guns blazing and shoot the young man who'd captured his sister's heart online—even though that would end everything.

That was too tempting to be considering it much longer.

When he got home, he made a sandwich for lunch and took it out to his balcony. He kicked his feet up on the railing and pulled his computer into his lap. Before delving into research on the Guardino family and Mia's father, he checked his phone. Nothing from Vegas on the condition of Coleman and nothing from Mia.

Her actions and behavior in light of this new information about her background made a lot of sense. He'd wanted to comfort her, take her in his arms and show her how much he cared about her...trauma. Instead, he'd come off as an ass, accusing her of wanting to set up his sister—even though she did.

If this were his case and Sabrina was his witness, he'd see the sense in the plan. He couldn't get past his own fear of putting Sabrina in danger—not that she hadn't done a good job of that herself.

He flipped open his laptop and dug up Mia's history. The Feds had efficiently wiped out a lot of what occurred, but with Mia's account of things, he could read between the lines of the reports.

She must've been terrified on so many levels wearing a wire with her boyfriend. Michael Guardino might not have been as besotted and oblivious as Nick Carlucci apparently was. He might've killed Mia right then and there.

With a crick in his neck, Billy transferred his laptop to the glass cocktail table and picked up the second half of his turkey sandwich. He stood up, stretched and then bellied up to the railing around his balcony and gazed at the boats in the marina.

Gus, one of the boat owners Billy had met, looked up and waved. Billy waved back. Gus didn't live on his boat like a few of the people Billy had met, but he spent a good part of each week at the marina.

A dark shape scurrying along the gangplank caught Billy's attention. The transient ducked out of sight before Billy could get a good look at him. Gus had told him a few homeless people had wandered to the marina to take advantage of some of the open boats to spend a night or two. Billy could understand how that might be preferable to the streets—unless you had a setup like Pierre. Who knows? Maybe Pierre had saved Bri's life—that time. At least he picked up her phone.

The breeze from the water gave Billy a sudden chill, and he stepped back inside the condo. Nick had been using Bri to bait Sabrina, and look what had happened to Bri. These people were ruthless. Mia had as good as admitted that the Carluccis would kill Nick to keep him quiet.

Maybe that was the move—lead the Carluccis to Nick. Once they got rid of him, Sabrina would be free. She had no information on the family other than Nick's murder of Ray Mayberry, and they knew it. If she'd had anything else, she would've already given it to the Feds.

Could he give up a killer to what would be his certain death? If it saved his sister, he could look the other way when it came to the morality of that decision. Of course, he didn't have a chance to test himself, as he had no clue about Nick's location.

He checked the time. The boys should be home from school about now and not quite ready for Little League practice. A pang of grief hit him behind the eyes. He'd played ball himself and had been teaching the boys how to throw and hit. They'd have to go through this season without his instruction.

After he had a video chat with the boys and cleaned up the kitchen, Billy sat down, cradling his phone. Still nothing from Mia. Should he call her? Telling him her story had wrung her out. He shouldn't have left her alone after that.

The phone buzzed in his hand, and he checked the display. His pulse ratcheted up a notch when he saw Brandon's number. The kid worked fast.

"Brandon, tell me you have something."

"I do." He clicked some keys in the background as if working to the last second. "I have some printouts of text messages and phone calls. I can't trace any of the numbers to a person, as they're all burner phones. I was able to get some locations on a few of these phones, though. Might help you find the subject."

"It absolutely will. You're a genius, my man. Are any of the text messages useful or incriminating?"

"Yeah, hold off on the genius compliment. The texts are vague—times and locations mostly, almost written in code."

"That's something. You were able to bypass that password, right? I'll be able to use that phone and pretend to be the phone's owner."

"I don't see why not. You wanna pick up the phone and the printouts today? I'm leaving pretty soon, but we can meet away from the station on my way home."

"Where is home? Don't you live closer to me in the marina than the Northeast Division in the Valley?"

"Not exactly close, but on the way. I live in Little Saigon with my parents, out by Garden Grove."

"Brandon, dude. You still live with your parents? Doesn't that seriously cramp your style with the ladies?"

"Yeah, well, traditional Vietnamese family, man. Doesn't mean I don't know a lot of girls with their own places."

"See? Genius. Just veer off toward the marina on your way home, and I'll get the stuff from you. I owe you, Brandon."

"Yeah, I know. I'll have to think about that."

When they ended the call, Billy tapped Mia's name.

She answered after the first ring. "Hi, Billy. What do you have?"

He blinked. She didn't sound destroyed. "My guy at the station got into Bri's phone."

"Excellent."

"SMPD didn't release Bri's name, correct?"

"They're still trying to track down her next of kin. They also don't want to alert her killers that they were successful, so yeah, her name's not out there. Neither is the nature of the crime."

"That means we can pretend to be her on the phone. We can try to get together with her contact, or maybe even Nick."

"We can do that. Do you have the phone now?"

"No, Brandon is dropping it off in about an hour on his way home from work. That gives you time to get here before he does."

"That sounds like the best plan I've heard all day. I'll be there before Brandon."

"Are you okay? You seemed kind of shaky when I dropped you off. I should've…"

"You should've done nothing. I'm fine. Went to the gym at the hotel, and then I got a massage. I feel brand-new."

She didn't need him to put her back together. She had her own methods.

"A massage sounds so good right now."

"Someone had to get to work—glad it was you. I'll see you in an hour."

Precisely an hour later, he buzzed Mia up to his place. She sailed in wearing black jeans, low-heeled black boots, a dark T-shirt that clung to her in all the right places and a hoodie tossed over her arm.

"You look ready for…" He waved a hand up and down her dark ensemble.

"Anything?" She kicked up one heel. "Debated between these boots and running shoes, but decided you could do the running if it came to that."

"The massage seems to have done you good."

She tilted her head. "Did you expect me to break down after telling you my sad story? I was more concerned that you believed I was ready to sacrifice your sister just because I had to risk it all."

"I know that's not the case." He hooked a thumb in his front pocket. "Putting myself on the outside, I can see that using Sabrina to reel in Nick is a good strategy, one I'd suggest myself, if…"

"If she weren't your sister. I get it." She ran her hands through her dark wavy hair. "We may not even get that opportunity. She hasn't made an appearance yet. Maybe she fooled everyone and headed east. Would she go to any of your other siblings? Your mother?"

"No way." He shook his head. "Wouldn't want to put them in any danger. She'd know I could handle it."

"Then LA it is." She went to his sliding glass door and flattened her hands against it. "Somewhere out there."

Billy slapped his hand against the buzzing phone in his back pocket. "Must be Brandon."

When he verified that Brandon was in front of the building, both he and Mia made their way to the street.

Brandon opened the passenger window of his Tesla, and Billy whistled. "Nice wheels."

Brandon grinned. "Perks of living with your parents, dude."

Billy jerked his thumb at Mia. "Mia, this is Brandon. Brandon, Mia. Don't ask."

"Wasn't going to." Brandon thrust a manila envelope out the open window. "It's all here."

"Thanks again, Brandon."

When they got upstairs, Billy shook out the contents of the envelope onto his kitchen table. The phone with the cracked screen slid out and spun around.

Mia grabbed the printouts and stacked them in order. She ran her finger down the list of numbers. "There are a few that are the most common. They are the ones with the text messages."

"What do those texts say?"

"Let's see." Mia shook out the page and read aloud. "Benny's at seven. No. Don't call. Nothing. Hotel at four. IDK. Not yet. A bunch of thumbs-up emojis from her contact."

Billy rolled his eyes. "Not much content there, but Brandon did warn me."

"Calls reveal no content." She tapped the pages. "These texts do. They were careful."

"Bri is dead. They weren't that careful." He dragged one of the pages toward him with a finger. "He'll probably get suspicious if we text him some long message. That's not their style."

"I just hope word didn't get back to him somehow that Bri was murdered. He did call her after the shooting this morning." She tapped one of the calls on the page. "The fact that she didn't call back has to be worrying him."

"If he did get the news, it wouldn't be from official sources. As far as the press is concerned, a tourist was involved in a robbery gone wrong."

"We both know there are plenty of nonofficial sources. What if the guy Bri was meeting was a Carlucci plant, not an employee of Nick's? What if he set her up and now knows she's dead?"

"I guess we'll find out, won't we? Do you see another path forward at this point?"

"I do not, other than waiting around for your sister to contact you, and I don't think she's ready for that yet."

"Can you blame her with all this swirling around?" Billy circled his finger in the air for emphasis.

"No. Sabrina is street smart—now." Mia pushed her hair from her face. "That's one of the saddest outcomes of this whole thing. The Carluccis and the Feds robbed Sabrina of her innocence. You can call it stupid if you want, but Sabrina believed in true love and happy endings at one point. I guarantee you, she doesn't believe in all that anymore."

Billy studied Mia's face, her long dark lashes lowered, creating crescents on her cheeks. Was she talking about Sabrina or herself? Did she still believe in happily-ever-after?

He cupped the phone in his hand. "Let's take a chance. Let's set up a meeting with this guy. I'll look up Benny's. That seems to be a favorite of theirs. It should be on the Westside somewhere, as she was staying in Santa Monica."

"No need." She glanced up from the phone records. "Benny's is the bar I followed her to on that first night when she left your place."

"Perfect." He shoved the phone at her. "What do you think? Benny's at nine?"

"Sure. Allow me." She picked up the phone and tapped away. Then she turned it to face him to show him the message they agreed on. "Okay?"

"Hit Send."

She tapped the phone and blew out a breath. "Let's hope he accepts the meeting, no suspicions or questions asked."

"Is there a name in there? Did they ever address each other by their names?"

Her gaze trailed down the page. "Nope."

"He might recognize you, Mia. You'd better stay out of sight."

"If he even shows up." She fluffed up her hair. "Besides, I can change my look."

The phone between them dinged, and they looked at each other before glancing down at the display. Through the cracks on the screen, Billy saw the contact's response—a thumbs-up.

Chapter Thirteen

Mia's knees bounced as she sat next to Billy in his Mercedes, wrapping a strand of blond hair around her finger. "Are you sure we shouldn't sit together? He's not going to recognize me with this disguise."

"Maybe not, but he may recognize me, even with my hat on, and if he sees me with you, he might put two and two together. We don't want to give him a chance to bolt before I corner him in the bar." Billy flicked down his visor and tugged his Dodgers baseball cap lower on his forehead as he peered in the mirror.

Mia smeared some red lipstick on her lips. "I'll go in first and take a seat at the bar. I'll give you the signal we agreed upon when our guy walks in."

Billy held out his fist for a bump. "Got it, partner."

She rolled her eyes when her knuckles met his, but a warm feeling rushed through her body. She knew how close Billy and his partner were, so she took his statement as the highest compliment.

Tucking the locks from her blond wig behind her ear, she pushed into Benny's, ignoring the lively patio. The place had a dive atmosphere, but the young, hip crowd had discovered it, creating a mishmash of people. The classic '70s rock thumped through the speakers, and she took a seat at the mahogany bar.

Fewer people vied for the bartender's attention than on her previous visit, and she ordered a bottle of light beer as soon as she straddled the barstool.

Ten minutes later, Billy sauntered into the bar and grabbed a small table squeezed in next to the jukebox, his back to the door but facing her at the bar.

A waitress in short-shorts and a black rock band tee hustled to his table and took his order in a half dip.

Billy took out his phone—his own, as Mia had Bri's—to look occupied and keep his head down. She should probably do the same. As a single woman, she'd attracted the attention of a couple of men on the fringes even though she'd definitely dressed down for the occasion. Maybe blondes did have more fun.

She sipped her beer from the bottle, and one of her admirers pulled up the stool beside her. "Young lady like yourself, looks like you need company."

Her gaze flicked across the man's ruddy cheeks and sun tattoo on his neck. If she engaged, she wouldn't stand out to Bri's contact guy but might be inviting a hassle down the road. She could handle the hassle but couldn't risk being made.

She smacked down her bottle and smiled. "Molly, but just to warn you, I'm here to meet someone."

"Boyfriend? Husband?" He glanced at her bare ring finger. "He shouldn't keep you waiting. I'm Doug."

"Hey, Doug. I'm meeting someone from one of

those dating apps. You use those?" Keep him talking in a noncommittal way.

"Damn, I tried a few times, but the ladies I met didn't look nothing like you—or nothing like their pictures."

"Yeah, that's happened to me a few times, too." She glanced at Bri's phone. Their contact was a few minutes late. "Might be worth it, though, huh?"

"You wanna hear the funniest story about one of my meetups?" He smacked his meaty fist on the bar, as if he'd already reached the punchline.

"Sure, lay it on me, Doug. I got a few of my own." The door opened, and her gaze darted to the man walking in. She gave a little shake of her head in Billy's direction. "What happened?"

Doug launched into a typical catfish tale, complete with filters and shady photography. Mia smiled in the right places and even managed a chuckle or two, her eyes averting from Doug's face to the door every time it swung open.

As Doug's story ended but his snorting over it hadn't, the phone on the bar buzzed. Mia snatched it and squinted at the text message. Meet me out back.

Damn. He either suspected something or wanted to be careful. Either way, she couldn't go waltzing out back with her blond wig and expect to get anything out of him. Billy wouldn't have an opportunity to corner him in a public place, either. If she insisted he come into the bar, he'd know something was wrong.

She held up the phone to Doug. "That's my date, almost here. Probably not a great start if he sees me having a good time with you, Doug. Give me your number, and if it doesn't work out with him, I'll give you a call."

"That's all right, sweetheart." Doug downed the last of the beer in his mug and gave her a wink. "I gotta get home to the missus, anyway."

Mia breathed out the word *jerk* to his back and called to the bartender, "Do you have an alley out back or what?"

"Little parking lot for the staff and a few extra spaces, dumpsters."

"Streets on either side or dead end?"

"Washington on one side and small street on the other. You wanna park there or something? Probably no spaces left now."

"My friend's picking me up. Just want her to be able to pull out of traffic."

He tapped the bottle, not really caring about her reasons. "Another beer?"

"I'm still working on this one." She texted their predicament to Billy across the room and suggested they hem him in by each taking a street and springing a surprise on him as he exited the parking lot one way or the other.

Billy texted back that he'd go out first and take the smaller street, as it would be more likely for their suspect to sneak out that way when Bri didn't meet him.

Mia agreed with Billy and texted their contact that she'd meet him in five minutes. Out of the corner of her eye, she watched Billy toss some bills on the table and leave through the front door.

Bri's phone buzzed again with a thumbs-up.

She asked the bartender for a glass of water and downed it before settling the bill. Then she hopped off the stool and followed in Billy's wake.

Moist air sprinkled her face when she landed on the sidewalk. Two women in high heels came tottering down the sidewalk to the bar's entrance, but Billy had already made his turn to the left to stake out the side street.

Mia walked the other way toward the busier street and turned the corner. She spotted the driveway to the small parking lot behind Benny's and the hair salon, now closed.

Pressing her back against the stucco wall of the bar, she crept toward the opening to the lot. A few cars rushed past her on the left, and a bus rumbled by, its closing doors squealing.

As the exhaust from the bus engulfed her, she coughed. Before she could catch her breath, the hard barrel of a gun jabbed her in the ribs.

A low, harsh voice grated in her ear. "Who the hell are you and where's Bri?"

BILLY PEEKED AROUND the corner of the building that housed a low-rent hair salon, squinting into the darkness of the small parking lot with buckled pavement and trash heaped beside a dumpster. His heart skipped a beat—empty.

If the bald guy knew this was a setup, he'd want to be in this space to find out who was setting him up—or he'd be watching this space as he and Mia were doing. This meeting would be too valuable to him and his boss. He wouldn't be a no-show.

Where would he be?

Billy tipped his head back to scan the rooftops of the neighboring buildings. As if sensing his gaze, a pigeon stirred.

He cranked his head over his shoulder, but the street had nothing but parked cars lining it.

A sharp cry made his blood run cold. That was no pigeon. The noise muffled by the fog carried across the parking lot, and he ducked, close to the wall.

Two figures emerged from the other side of the lot—the side he'd sent Mia to cover. A man with a dark jacket and bald head gleaming under the streetlamp dragged Mia into the parking lot. Billy couldn't see the gun in the man's hand, but he had one arm around Mia's chest and the other shoved into her side. It didn't take a genius to figure out he had her at gunpoint.

While the man forced Mia to the other side of the dumpster away from the street, Billy's instincts kicked in.

Hunched over, he ran along the wall, the soles of his tennis shoes whispering along the asphalt as he took cover between the cars parked in the slots. Gun drawn, he sprang into the open. "Drop your gun."

Both the man and Mia jerked their heads toward him. Mia used the distraction to elbow her captor in the chin before ducking and launching her body against the man's legs.

He staggered, his gun still clutched in his hand. If

he aimed that weapon at Mia, Billy would drop him where he stood. "Freeze. Drop the gun and nobody gets hurt. Do you really want to shoot a US marshal or an LAPD homicide detective?"

"He has my weapon, too, Billy."

"Slide both of those guns toward me. We just wanna talk. That's all." Billy moved close enough to see a sheen of sweat break out on the man's forehead. "What's your name?"

The man answered, "Beckett. Where's Bri? Is she dead? Was that her at the hotel today?"

Billy took another step closer. "Bri's dead, Beckett. It wasn't us. I think you know who it was."

"Damn it." Beckett switched his hold on the gun, gripping the barrel. He placed it on the ground and slid it toward Billy.

"Where's my partner's weapon?"

"It's in his pocket." Mia half rose from her crouch and said, "I'm taking it now, Beckett."

She slid her hand into Beckett's pocket as he spread his arms out to his sides. Once she secured the gun, she moved to Billy's side, picking up Beckett's gun on the way. Billy felt a slight tremble run through her body as she stood next to him.

"Let's go back inside and get a drink. I think we could all use one." Billy holstered his gun. "Just don't try to run. We could get you in serious trouble with the Carluccis, if they don't already know about you. Do they?"

Beckett shook his head. "I don't work for them."

"We know that. Let's talk about your options— inside."

They made a strange-looking procession, walking single file on the sidewalk back to the front of Benny's, Beckett leading the way with three guns behind him, if not aimed at him.

Benny's buzzed with even more activity on their return trip, but Billy was able to snag the table by the jukebox again. He herded Beckett into the chair against the wall, while he and Mia hemmed him in by taking the seats across from him.

"Tell us what's going on with Nick Carlucci." Billy had to hunch forward so Beckett could hear him, but the music from the jukebox provided cover for their conversation.

Beckett licked his lips. "How do I know you are who you say you are? How do I know you're not working for the Carlucci family?"

Billy growled. "Because you'd be dead by now."

Mia hit her leg against his under the table and pulled her badge from her purse. "I'm Mia Romano, US Marshals Service."

Cupping his own badge in his hand, Billy said, "Detective Billy Crouch, LAPD Homicide, but then you know that."

Beckett swallowed. "You're Sabrina's brother."

"Yeah, so you can understand why I'm…interested in what you have to say. So start talking."

The same waitress as before with The Who T-shirt tossed some cocktail napkins onto the table. "What can I get you?"

They all ordered bottled beer, but Billy had no intention of imbibing. When the waitress turned, Billy drilled his finger into the table. "Go."

"I work for Nick, not the family. Nick's not gonna hurt Sabrina. I swear to God. He loves that girl."

Billy flinched, and a muscle throbbed at the corner of his mouth. "Do you know where Nick is?"

"Not right this minute." Beckett's beady eyes shifted right and left. "I'm supposed to locate Sabrina and either bring her to him or let him know where she is. Or, I mean, Bri was supposed to do that. I was Bri's go-between."

Mia asked, "Did Nick's family hide him after the Ray-May murder?"

"They did at first, but Nick couldn't stand it anymore. He broke free."

"The family is looking for him now?" Billy spread his hands on the table, his thumbs touching.

"Yeah, that's why they went after Coleman. Bri thought she'd send you to Vegas to get you out of LA and to ruffle the Carlucci feathers." Beckett ran a thumb over his brow bone, and Billy realized the guy didn't have eyebrows, either. "None of us thought the Carluccis would go after Coleman. It was at that point Nick realized his family was serious about locating him."

"Why wouldn't they be?" Mia pulled a napkin in front of her as the waitress delivered their drinks.

"Keep a tab open?"

"This is it." Billy pulled out his wallet. He didn't need the waitress interrupting them every ten minutes.

Tracing a finger around the rim of her beer bottle, Mia said, "If the Feds pick up Nick, they're not going to question him only about the Ray-May murder. They have a litany of crimes they're itching to solve—and Nick's just the guy to help them. The Carluccis know that. Nick doesn't?"

"Nick is family. Nick and Vince are like this." Beckett crossed his fingers.

Billy murmured, "Fredo."

"What?" Beckett leaned forward, cupping his ear.

Mia snorted. "C'mon, Beckett. Nick has to realize that the family business is at stake. If Nick rats them out, the party is over."

"But that's just it." Beckett took a long pull from his beer. "Nick would never rat out the family, and Vince knows that. He's looking for Nick to protect him, protect him against himself."

Billy slammed his fist against the table, rattling the bottles, as a guitar solo wailed from the speakers. "Does Nick also realize that my sister is nothing to the Carluccis? If they find her before Nick does, it's all over for Sabrina, too."

"Nick does know that. That's why he's trying to find her, to protect her. If he can get her to go with him to South America, he can keep her away from his family and they can be together."

"Wait, wait." Mia waved her hands over the table. "Why is Nick so sure Sabrina will welcome him with open arms?"

"You don't know?" Beckett cocked his head as

he dragged a fingernail through the foil label on his beer bottle.

"I'm not in the habit of asking questions when I already know the answers." Mia ran a hand through her blond wig.

Beckett slid a glance toward Billy, and Billy found himself gripping the edge of the table.

"Well?" Billy barked so loudly the couple on the other side of the jukebox glanced up from their conversation.

Beckett brought his shoulders up to his ears. "Because she said she would. That's why she left witness protection."

Chapter Fourteen

The roaring in Billy's ears drowned out all the noise from the bar, and he almost lunged across the table. "You lying piece of…"

"Whoa." Mia put a hand on his arm. "Stop. Let's talk this through."

"There's nothing to talk about." The sudden pain in his skull had Billy reaching for the beer in front of him. "He's lying. Sabrina would never agree to meet with a killer."

"I understand. She would if she truly loved him." Mia had accompanied these infuriating words with a hard squeeze to his knee.

She didn't believe it, did she? Her love for her fiancé, Michael, hadn't deterred her from doing the right thing, and Michael Guardino hadn't even killed anyone—yet.

"Yeah, yeah." Beckett nodded enthusiastically. "You get it. They love each other. There's been no one else for Nick all these years in hiding."

"Let's slow down a minute." Mia ran her fingers, damp from her beer bottle, along Billy's knotted forearm. "Have Nick and Sabrina been in touch all this time?"

"Only in the past year. She reached out to Nick through this online gaming community."

"*She* reached out to *him*." Billy crossed his arms over his chest and puffed it out, wanting to do violence to something—or somebody.

"Nick had been waiting for years. They played that online game together after they met on a dating site but before they met in person. They were both big fans." Beckett scratched his hairless arms.

"What gaming site, Beckett?" Mia cupped her chin in her palm, as if she and Beckett were besties.

"I… I don't want to tell you that, some game with knights and dragons. It's their way to communicate." Beckett clasped his hands around his beer bottle, lacing his fingers.

"Then why haven't they?" Billy's nostrils flared as he caught the chink in Beckett's story. "If Sabrina is so eager to meet up with Nick after all these years, why hasn't she done so? Why did Nick have to send Bri out to find her? Send you?"

Beckett coughed. "We don't know. At the beginning, Nick thought his family had gotten to her, but they've shown their hand, haven't they? They're still looking for her, too."

"She could've changed her mind, then. Maybe she doesn't want anything to do with Nick. Maybe she's hiding from him." The muscle in Billy's jaw finally relaxed since the moment Beckett started spewing his lies.

"The question I have, Beckett—" Mia slid her untouched beer toward him "—is what does Nick plan to do if Sabrina did change her mind about him?"

"He just won't let himself believe that." Beckett downed the rest of his drink and reached for Mia's. "But either way, he's not going to hurt her. He'd never do that or let his family hurt her."

Billy exhaled noisily from his nose. Beckett and Nick were a couple of naive morons, but their naivete was putting his sister's life at risk.

"What's gonna happen to me? I didn't do nothing wrong."

Mia flicked the strands of her wig. "You pulled a gun on two law enforcement officers."

He spread his hands. "I didn't mean to. I mean, I thought you were the Carluccis come to kill me. It was self-defense."

If Billy had his way, he'd slap cuffs on this guy right now, but Mia's blue eyes were alive with some plan.

She folded her hands in front of her. "I can see that. Also, if you're trying to protect Sabrina from the Carluccis, that's what we want, too."

Billy clenched his teeth to keep his jaw from dropping. He'd let her work this plan.

"But know this." She leveled a finger a Beckett. "If we find her first, I'm going to do everything in my power to get her back into WITSEC, and the Feds are going to keep looking for Nick."

"I… I…" Beckett's gaze bounced between Billy's face and Mia's, and Billy tried his damnedest to keep his blank. "I can't tell Nick I met with you. He'd wonder about my loyalty."

"I got that." Mia scooted her chair back. "Now get the hell out of here before I change my mind."

Billy's shock matched Beckett's, but he was marginally able to control it better.

Beckett jumped from his chair, almost knocking it over. "My gun?"

Mia gave him a long stare from narrowed eyes. "You're kidding."

"Yeah, yeah, I am." In his haste to get away, Beckett stumbled, his foot hitting the leg of the small table, and Billy's hand shot out to grab his tottering half-full bottle.

He watched the back of Beckett as he scurried out of the bar, and then he turned to Mia. "You wanna tell me what that's all about? Maybe we could've used Beckett to lure Nick out of hiding."

Mia dragged the wig from her head and tossed it into the chair recently vacated by Beckett. She dug her fingers into her hair and massaged her scalp. "Oh, no, we're gonna use someone else to lure Nick out of hiding—your sister."

MIA BRACED FOR the expected explosion by gripping both ends of the table and holding her breath. Billy didn't disappoint.

He slapped both hands on the table and growled. "The hell you are."

'Hear me out." She held up one finger, but since

Billy looked ready to bite it off, she snatched it back. "Sabrina's already setting him up."

"What are you talking about?" The poor man rubbed his forehead, and she just wanted to take his face in her hands and kiss his mouth.

"I'm telling you right now, Billy. There is no way Sabrina contacted Nick to run away with him. No way. Nick destroyed any feelings she had for him when he shot Ray." She scooted forward in her chair, putting her face closer to his. "Think about it. Why would she wait close to four years to rekindle the romance?"

"I don't know." He shook his head. "She got lonely?"

"Where do you think we had her stashed all this time? She's been living her life. She finished college and passed her CPA exam. She has friends and she goes on dates. She's not sitting around pining for the guy who separated her from her family. A guy who's in the mob. A guy who murdered someone in cold blood."

He rubbed his eye. "Then why? Why now?"

"She misses you. She misses her family. She knows her father died, and she doesn't want to lose her mother, too."

"What do you think she's planning?"

"Exactly what I told you. She's planning to set up Nick, get him arrested. Once she testifies against him, she'll be done. As clueless as Beckett is, he did get something right."

"What's that?" Billy took another slug from his beer. He probably needed it—and about five more.

"Nick is not going to testify against his family. He might admit to the Ray-May murder, he might try to fight it, but he's not going to implicate his brother in any mob crimes. No way. Once Nick is convicted, the family will have no reason to go after Sabrina. She can't harm them in any way. Sabrina is orchestrating her freedom." She winked at him. "I told you she was street savvy now."

Billy slumped in his chair, stretching his long legs in front of him. "Just because she's willing to use herself as bait, it doesn't mean we have to play along."

"I don't think we have a choice, big brother. The woman of the hour has made a decision, and it's up to us to go along with it and keep her as safe as possible."

"How are we going to do that?"

"I'm giving you a break here, Cool Breeze. Because your sister is involved, you're not thinking like a detective. We're going to get to Sabrina ourselves before anyone else does."

He hit the side of his head with the heel of his hand. "You're right. My brain is fogged in, and it has nothing to do with this beer. How exactly are we going to reach Sabrina when we haven't been able to do that yet?"

"Beckett gave us the key." She grabbed his hand. "C'mon. You into gaming?"

BY THE TIME they got back to Billy's condo, Mia had told him everything she knew about the gaming world.

As he yanked his laptop from the charger, he said, "You don't strike me as a gamer type. You're too…"

"Old?" She jabbed him in the ribs as he sat next to her on the couch.

"Normal."

"Tons of people are into gaming today—and I'm not that normal." She dragged his computer into her lap. "My youngest sister is a gamer. That's why I knew exactly what game Beckett meant when he mentioned the medieval knights and dragons."

"Don't they all have knights and dragons?" His shoulder pressed against hers, and she wriggled away a few inches. He'd have to keep his distance if she wanted to concentrate.

"A few do, but Castles and Crosses has been the most popular for a while now. They have to be using that to communicate. I figure if Sabrina's gaming on that site to reach Nick, we should be able to get in touch with her, too."

Billy folded his arms, bunching his fists into his biceps. "How do you know for sure Sabrina is setting up Nick instead of planning to take off with him?"

"I know it here." She patted her chest. "And you should, too."

"I thought I knew my sister, but I never would've suspected she'd be on a sugar daddy website and then actually take off to meet someone without telling me."

She tapped on his keyboard to search for the Castles and Crosses game. "That's because you're her brother, not her BFF. She didn't even tell most of her friends about Nick, didn't mention him to Rissa, who was even in on the dating app. She wasn't going to tell you."

He nodded toward his TV. "Don't you usually play those games on the TV?"

"Usually, but you don't have a gaming console or remote, so the computer is the next best thing." She brought up the site on Billy's laptop. "Besides, we're not going to be entering duels or scaling castle walls. We're going to be creeping around looking at players and their profiles."

"This is a weird world." He pushed up from the couch. "Do you want something to drink?"

She glanced up from her typing. "I'll take a glass of that white we had the other night with the Chinese food."

Her fingers faltered on the keyboard. That white wine had caused her to throw caution to the wind that night. Maybe she needed that liquid courage again.

He opened the fridge door. "That sounds good. I wanted to down that beer in Benny's when Beckett told me Sabrina had been in contact with Nick, but I still had to drive home."

"I noticed your great restraint. I wanted to kick you under the table again to let you know that you didn't have to worry."

He returned to the living room carrying two glasses of wine. "I've been worried ever since Bri walked into my life."

She blew out a breath and pinched the stem of the wineglass between her fingers. "Okay, I set up an account for you with the username Cool Breeze. Sabrina knows your nickname, right?"

"Yeah, now what?"

"We wait a few minutes until your account is approved, and then you start entering some of the rooms and make a splash."

"You mean, *you* enter some rooms, whatever that means. I don't know what to do to cause a splash."

"That's just it. You're a newbie. You stumble around, get into people's games, get on their nerves. Get yourself talked about. Sabrina's not going to find you if you keep a low profile."

"Do we have to wait for her to find us again? That hasn't been working out too well so far." He clasped the back of his neck.

"I'm sure she's not playing as Sabrina or even Chanel, but just like you, she might be using a moniker you'll recognize. Did she have a nickname as a kid?"

"We used to call her Stick because she was tall and skinny." Billy's lips curled into a smile at the memory, and Mia's heart ached for him.

"Who knows? Maybe we'll find a Stick." She tapped the monitor. "We've been approved. Start setting up your profile."

Billy spent the next several minutes designing a knight in black shining armor with a variety of badges.

Mia rested her chin on his shoulder. "That is so you."

"Now what?" He turned slightly and the rough scruff of his chin brushed her cheek.

"Go to the different areas and play. I'll be watching the other player names. We can also check past players in the room."

Billy clicked into an embattled castle first and proceeded to challenge everyone to a duel. His keyboard hindered his movements, but he wasn't half-bad.

"You're getting the hang of it." She clasped his fingers. "Hold on. Let's check out the users before you move to the forest."

She read the names out loud to him, and he shook his head at each one.

He drummed his fingers impatiently on the edge of the laptop. "Can we go to the forest now?"

"I think I've just turned you into a gaming nerd." She bumped his arm. "Go on."

Billy continued to stumble his way through the gaming landscape as Mia scrolled through the users.

"Onto the sea!" Billy pumped his fist.

Mia downed the last of her wine and held up her glass. "Do you want a refill?"

"No, no. I need to keep my wits sharp." He cracked his knuckles. "I think I'm going to buy my boys a gaming console before they come to stay this summer."

Mia grinned in the kitchen as she splashed more wine into her glass. "The old buy-it-for-the-kids ploy. I guarantee, if you get into gaming with your sons, Cool Breeze will become Cool Dad."

"Another excellent reason to buy one." He sucked in a breath as she sat next to him. "Someone blocked me from blowing up that ship."

"Ready to check out the next location? You still

have the King's Road to decimate, and that's a popular area."

"I think I'll be good at that one."

"Users first." She hovered over the users on display, reading the names aloud as Billy geared up for his next assault.

"Nope, nope, nope." Billy rubbed his eyes.

"I'll check the history." She ran the cursor down each username. "Mad Dog, Theon, Sun Devil, Dolphin Girl, Lil Peg..."

"Wait!" Billy grabbed her arm. "Dolphin Girl?"

Mia's heart fluttered. "Does that mean something to you?"

Billy leaned in, squinting at the username and the blue dolphin character with a pink crown. "Sabrina always loved dolphins and..."

"And she has a dolphin tattoo on her shoulder." Mia bounced in her seat.

"She didn't have that before she left, at least I don't think she did, but Bri told me about it when I asked her to describe Sabrina, and it made sense." He poised one unsteady finger over the dolphin. "Do you think that could be her?"

With her heart pounding, Mia said, "Let me do a little research."

She clicked on Dolphin Girl's profile and swore. "She has her profile set to private."

"Does that mean we can't send her a message?" Billy's shoulders sagged as he collapsed against the couch.

"No." She tapped the message icon. "She accepts

private messages. She'd have to if she wants to keep the lines of communication open with Nick."

Billy jolted forward. "I can send her a message? I can send my sister a message?"

"If this is your sister. We don't even know that yet, Billy." She didn't want him to get his hopes up, but this was as close as they'd gotten to finding her.

"I have a feeling—a good feeling for a change." He settled the laptop on the coffee table in front of them. "What should I write? Can anybody else see this message?"

"No, so it doesn't have to be in code or anything, but you want her to know it's you. She might be afraid that one of the Carlucci family found out about this line of communication. It should be something only your family knows."

"Her nickname never went out of family circles. That's for sure—and neither did our father's. Unless she told someone, those would be a safe bet."

"Go for it."

As he typed out the message to Dolphin Girl, Mia read it aloud. "Stick, contact me. I can help you. The Colonel sends his love."

He asked, "Sound good?"

"I think that'll work. Hit Send."

He sent the message and then stared at the display. "How long?"

"She hasn't even read it yet. We have no idea how often she's on here. It might be a while, but Brandon, your tech guy, might be able to get an IP address from the company if they play ball. If they don't, we can make them."

"Okay." He dragged his gaze away from the screen and met her eyes with his own. "Thanks."

"We'll find her." She took both of his hands in hers. "You called your father the Colonel?"

Billy cracked a smile. "Yeah, he'd been in the army and ran our household with military precision. We used to snicker behind his back, but never to his face. Only Sabrina could tease him. She was the baby and could do no wrong in my father's eyes. He died with a broken heart."

"We can do this, Billy. She can do it." She stroked his arm. "Are you still opposed to her luring Nick with promises she has no intention of keeping?"

"If you could do it, she can. And we'll help her." He laced his fingers through hers, the light and dark of their skin tones creating a pleasing pattern.

She raised their conjoined hands to her lips. "I'll do anything to help her—and you. You know that."

"Because she's your witness and I'm her brother."

She straddled him, as she'd done the night before, and linked her arms around his neck. "Because she's my witness, and you're the hottest man I've had the pleasure of partnering with...ever."

"Has to be someone you partner with?" He cocked his head and encircled her waist with his hands.

"I wanna make sure my man has my back. What better way to test him?" She dipped her head and slanted her mouth across his.

"Have I passed the test?" He ran a thumb along her lower lip, still throbbing from their kiss.

She widened her eyes. "Did you think that was the only test?"

"I was hoping it wasn't." His lips spread into a smile. "I'm up for another test. I mean, I'm literally up for it."

A thrill ran down her spine, and they both went in for a kiss at the same time, bumping noses.

"Ooh, I failed that test. Here." He took her face in his hands, and tilting his head, he caressed her lips with his.

As he deepened the kiss, she dug her fingers into his short hair, her nails reaching his scalp.

He drew back sharply, and her stomach plunged. Was he having second thoughts? She flattened her hand against his chest. "What's wrong?"

"I'm going to have to head to the bedroom to get some protection. We can always continue this romp in there."

"Hang on." She wriggled to the edge of the couch and dragged her purse toward her. She upended it on the floor and pawed through the contents. Her fingers stumbled across a foil-wrapped square, and she held the condom up in the air. "Just in case."

If Billy objected to the idea of her carrying condoms in her purse, his smile didn't reflect it. "All systems go."

He snatched the condom from her fingers and shifted his body, taking her down to a horizontal position. His hands pulled at her shirt, yanking it over her head in one deft move. He definitely had practice removing women's clothing, and she didn't mind one bit.

She slipped her arms from the straps of her bra. "A little help here."

He complied by unhooking her bra and then immediately dragging his own shirt over his head to press his chest against hers. His warm skin enflamed her desire, which he stoked even more by kissing her again and slipping his tongue into her mouth.

She stroked his smooth back and exhaled in his ear. "So perfect."

As he nudged her onto her back, he said, "I never thought you'd be so easy to please."

"Everything about you pleases me, so you don't have to try too hard." She fumbled with his belt and yanked at the zipper of his black jeans. "But no slacking. I still want you to do your very best."

He lifted his hips to allow her to pull down his jeans and black briefs all at once. The undressing stopped at his knees, and he braced himself above her with one arm as he undid her pants and tugged them down her hips.

He didn't have the patience to wait until they were fully naked. He slid one hand beneath her derriere, tilting her hips forward, and buried his head between her legs. His hair tickled her thighs, and she gasped somewhere between laughter and passion as his tongue met her flesh.

She draped her legs over his shoulders and dug her fingernails into his arm as he continued to tease her toward her climax. She cried out with her release, and he kissed a path from her mound to her mouth.

As she still gasped from the downward path of the roller coaster, he slipped on the condom with no help from her. He entered her, urging her to new, dizzying heights of passion. She hooked one leg around his slim hips in an attempt to draw him closer, as if she couldn't quite get him close enough.

She still had so many things she wanted to do to his body, but the rhythm of his thrusts signaled his impatience. Hell, they had the rest of the night, and presumably, he had more protection in his bedroom. She didn't want to distract him from his single-minded goal, so she clawed at his muscular backside to urge him to his own climax.

After one particularly deep plunge, Billy seemed to freeze. Then his body shuddered, and his eyes flew open to stare into hers as he sailed toward the finish line.

His thrusts slowed to a gentle rocking, and she caught a bead of sweat rolling down his chiseled chest with the tip of her finger. "I need more."

"Glad to hear it. I do have a bedroom with a bed and everything."

"I'm sure you do, but I couldn't wait that long."

As he cupped her breast and dipped his head to run his tongue around her nipple, the laptop on the coffee table dinged.

Mia fell halfway off the couch as she scrambled to grab the computer. Panting as much from their recent exertion as their current excitement, they hunched forward to peer at the display, the Castles and Crosses game still flickering on the screen.

She clicked on the message icon for Cool Breeze and sucked in a sharp breath. "There it is. You have a message from Dolphin Girl."

Chapter Fifteen

Billy's hand trembled as he took control of the mouse
from Mia and clicked on the message.

Mia breathed into his ear. "What does it say?"

He read aloud. "I've been holding off because of
your 'guests.' I do this my way."

Gripping the top of the laptop, Billy dropped his
head. Reading the first words from Sabrina in five
years when he'd thought she was dead overwhelmed
him. For a second, he couldn't breathe. Couldn't
think. Couldn't speak.

Mia rubbed a circle on his back with her hand.
Where she'd been clawing and clutching at him in
passion just a few minutes ago, her touch was now
gentle, soothing. She kissed the side of his neck. "It's
really her."

"She sounds so—" he swiped the back of his hand
across his nose "—impersonal, hard. Are we sure it's
her? What if it's Nick Carlucci trying to draw me out,
trying to get to Sabrina?"

"I doubt that, but if you're concerned, you can try
to verify her identity just like you ID'd yourself to
her with words only she would know."

"As much as I want to dive right in here, we need to be cautious—for Sabrina's sake." He yanked up his jeans and wiped his hands on his denim-covered thighs. He typed a message back to Dolphin Girl and held his breath.

She replied almost immediately, and Billy's muscles finally uncoiled as he relaxed against the cushions of the couch.

Mia leaned forward. "The walls of her bedroom were painted lavender?"

"When her older sisters left home for college and she finally got her own room, she requested purple walls. My mom thought it was a hideous color and kept pressuring my dad to put off painting it, so I came home and painted it for her. It wasn't half-bad. This is Sabrina."

"Now that you two have vetted each other, set up the meeting. If the guest she's worried about is me, let her know I'm on board for whatever she wants to do at this point. I think she's afraid I'm going to haul her back into WITSEC."

"And I'm afraid you won't." Billy massaged the back of his neck. "Where should we meet her? I have to believe this place is being watched."

"I agree. Let her set the schedule. She's done an excellent job of staying under the radar so far."

"Okay." He raised an eyebrow at her as he dragged the computer into his lap. "Maybe you could put your top on. I'm trying to concentrate here."

She pressed her lips against his shoulder and pulled on her clothes as he typed a new message to Sabrina.

Poking Mia in the back as she fumbled with her bra, he said, "I wrote, 'Tell me when and where, and I'll meet you and make sure we're not followed.'"

Her head popped out of the top of her T-shirt. "That's wide open."

Sabrina sent a one-word message back. We?

"Told ya." Mia slugged his bicep.

He read the words as he entered them. "Mia will listen to you. Trust her. I do."

She hung her arm around his neck. "I trust you, too, Detective Crouch, but I hope Sabrina believes you."

Another ding signaled Sabrina's response, and Billy chuckled. "She put a little eye-rolling emoji and told me to accept the next invitation I received."

"I told you she was savvy." She pushed up from the couch. "Water? You wore me out and then discarded me."

"We practically pushed each other out of the way to get to that laptop." He came up behind her in the kitchen and lifted her hair from the back of her neck, placing a kiss at the top of her spine. "That's not how I wanted our encounter to end. Let's go to bed and continue our…exploration. I feel like a great weight has been lifted from my shoulders now. I feel superhuman."

"I like the sound of that." She turned to face him, holding two glasses of water. "Sustenance before we do the deep dive."

"Deep dive?" He quirked his eyebrows up and down. "I like the sound of that."

This time when he took Mia to his bed, he explored

every inch of her beautiful body, and she insisted on returning the favor.

Had finding his sister alive at last freed him to trust and love again? Or was that all Mia?

THE FOLLOWING MORNING, Billy felt the bed next to him for the warm body that had stayed close to his all night long. His fingers met an expanse of cool sheets, and he sat up with a start, his heart pounding.

Some off-key singing from the kitchen soothed his nerves and brought a smile to his lips. She hadn't bolted.

He swung his legs off the bed and grabbed his briefs before padding out of the bedroom. Standing still for a few seconds, he enjoyed the view of Mia dancing around his kitchen in his T-shirt and nothing else, as far as he could tell, waving a spatula in the air.

"Is that your mic?"

She squealed and spun around, her mic dripping eggs onto the floor. "You scared me. Give a girl some warning—especially if you plan to prance around in your underwear."

"Prance?" He ate up the distance between them with a few long strides and grabbed her around the waist. "I don't prance."

Holding the spatula in the air, she kissed his mouth, the salty taste of bacon touching his lips.

"I thought you didn't eat red meat." He pinched her hip.

She covered her mouth, her eyes wide. "I don't,

usually. One end of the piece I was frying got a little too crispy, so I nipped it off."

He reached past her and snatched a piece of bacon from a row on a paper towel. "I like it crispy."

"Seems you like it a lot of ways." She slid her hand into his briefs and squeezed one cheek as he flexed it.

"Don't strike a match if you're not ready to burn down the kitchen." He ran a hand up her bare thigh beneath the T-shirt she'd stolen from his closet, and she shivered.

"Noted." She backed up to the kitchen counter, waving the spatula between them. "In addition to that bacon, I have scrambled eggs, toast and coffee. I'd hate to see it go to waste."

"I'll set the table after I grab some shorts." He tapped her nose. "If we're ever going to eat breakfast, I don't want to tempt you."

"You could be wearing a snowsuit, and you'd still tempt me, Cool Breeze." She turned back to the eggs on the stove. "And about that nickname—there was nothing cool about you last night. Hot, hot, hot."

He walked back to the bedroom with a stupid smile that felt permanently etched on his face. Finding out his sister was still alive had put it there, and Mia's presence in his place—in his life—was keeping it there.

He grabbed a pair of basketball shorts from his drawer and stepped into them, adjusting the elastic around his waist. Glancing at her clothes scattered across the bedroom floor, he considered asking Mia to make herself decent, but he kinda liked her indecent.

He charged back into the kitchen, and Mia tossed him a look over her shoulder. "I thought you were going to cover up. All that bare skin and those chiseled pecs are going to keep me salivating."

"You can always return my T-shirt." He raised one eyebrow in his best imitation of James Bond.

"You wish." She slid some eggs on two plates and snatched some toast from the toaster with her fingertips. "Breakfast is served."

Billy poured the coffee and put some silverware and napkins on the place mats. He hadn't felt this domestic since the boys left. He ducked into the fridge and held up a jar of salsa. "For your eggs?"

"Absolutely. The longer I'm in California, the more I have to eat the stuff on everything." She placed the food on the table.

He pulled her chair out for her. "We'll make an Angeleno out of you yet."

"From DC?" She took her seat and shook her napkin in her lap, avoiding his eyes.

Was that her way of reminding him that they lived on different sides of the country? He didn't need the reminder. Didn't want to think about it.

He picked up a piece of bacon and crumbled it into his scrambled eggs, mixing them together.

"What is that?" She pointed her fork at his plate.

"This is how my younger son eats scrambled eggs and bacon. It grew on me." He dug his fork into the mess.

"The younger one is Darius, right? James is the older?"

"You saw them at the wedding you crashed?" He snapped his fingers. "That's right. You researched me first. Were you going to just keep watching me without making contact?"

"Those were my orders, but just so you know, I was always in favor of telling you the truth. It's not like you were a civilian we couldn't trust." She crunched into a piece of toast and dabbed the crumbs from her mouth. "But then you made your move on Coleman, and I figured you really needed to know the situation."

"I'm glad you did—make contact, that is."

"Me, too, but I'm not sure the contact we had last night…"

"And this morning."

"…and this morning—" a pink blush spread on her cheeks "—was warranted."

"Oh, it was." He skimmed a knuckle down the side of her throat, and she swallowed. As much as he enjoyed their banter, they still had business to discuss— the business of meeting with Sabrina.

Mia must've had the same thought, because they both started talking at once.

"You first. Imma stuff my face and listen."

She poked at the eggs on her plate. "I was just going to ask you how you thought Sabrina would contact you…us."

He chewed, swallowed, took a sip of his coffee and sat back in his chair. "Her message advised me not to turn down any invitations, so I guess I should look out for an invite to something."

"An event?" Mia dumped some milk in her coffee. "Maybe she's planning to show up at a public event, a concert or something, to blend in with the crowd."

"I hope her musical tastes have changed in five years." He laced his fingers behind his head. "It has to be something natural. If I'm being watched, I can't do anything too unexpected."

"Like I said before, the girl has street smarts. Do you have some work you can do at home? I suggest you hang out here for the day."

"You think she'll make contact as early as today?"

"I think she's been waiting long enough."

"I can keep busy." He grabbed his fork and dug into his eggs and bacon. "What about you? Are you going to stick around or head back to your hotel?"

"It's already late, almost afternoon. I need to check in with Tucker." She pinched the material of his T-shirt and pulled it away from her body. "I also need to shower and change."

Disappointment made his next mouthful hard to swallow, but he couldn't expect her to sit around here all day. After the fireworks of last night, it might be best to scale things back in anticipation of her returning to her life in DC or her next case—provided this case went as planned.

Uneasiness settled in his gut again. The excitement of knowing Sabrina was okay and that he'd be able to see her soon had outweighed the dread he'd felt at her insistence of setting up Nick. Would she even be able to go through with that?

Mia covered his hand. "It'll be okay. Sabrina knows

what she's doing, and we'll guide her. We're both professionals with years of experience, and she's a young woman on a mission to take her life back. What could go wrong?"

"Don't get me started." He popped the last corner of his toast in his mouth and stood up, grabbing his plate. He held it out to her. "Are you done?"

She stacked her plate on top of his and folded her hands around her coffee mug as he took the dishes to the kitchen.

"I guess I'll get going." She stood up and sashayed to the bedroom. "Might just take this T-shirt with me, though."

Billy put the dishes in the dishwasher and washed the frying pan. He'd always done his fair share of the chores around the house when he'd been married to Sonia. She'd always claimed that he'd been great at sharing the housework, but not so great at sharing his emotions.

He'd kept his fears and guilt about Sabrina's disappearance to himself, but it had occupied his mind. Had made him approach every homicide case as if the dead were his sister. That perspective had made him a rock star at his job but a failure as a husband.

He took his coffee cup to his balcony and leaned over the railing to watch the boats slide in and out of the marina. Lost in thought, he didn't hear Mia come up behind him until she wrapped her arms around his waist.

"It's a beautiful day." She kissed his shoulder.

Drawing her next to him, he draped an arm around

her shoulders. "Beautiful start to a beautiful day. I just hope it has a happy ending."

She tapped his hand. "That man is waving to you. Do you think he needs help?"

Billy squinted at the boat slips and waved back to Gus hosing off the deck of his boat. "That's Gus. He keeps a boat down here."

"Looks like he has something to say to you. Maybe he does need some help."

Billy leaned over the railing of his balcony. "Hey, Gus."

Gus strode up to the lawn beneath the condo. The wiry man had an energetic gait and always seemed to be moving. Sitting on the deck of a boat seemed to Billy like an odd pastime for this man in perpetual motion.

"Hiya, Billy. Looks like you've been off work for a few days."

Billy's hands tightened on the wood. He should know that anyone's schedule could be an open book for perceptive people.

"Yeah, a little time off."

"Would you like to go sailing with me tonight? Call it a sunset cruise. Your lady friend can come along, too."

The last thing Billy wanted to do was go on a romantic sunset cruise with Mia…and Gus. He mumbled under his breath, "Hate to disappoint the old guy."

Mia grabbed his arm, digging her fingernails into his flesh. "Don't you dare refuse."

Billy jerked his head to the side. "Do you want to go?"

"Don't you get it?" Reaching up, she took his face in her hands. "This is the invitation we've been waiting for."

Chapter Sixteen

"You're sure? A boat? How does Sabrina know Gus?" A crease formed between his eyebrows.

"It's an invitation." Mia waved at the birdlike man below. "We'd love to go. Meet you at your boat?"

Gus gave them a thumbs-up and scurried back to the slip.

Billy shook his head. "I guess. If this isn't Sabrina, we're gonna feel stupid sailing along with Gus, wasting our evening."

"Think about it, Billy. A boat is perfect. She knows nobody is going to be following us on a sailboat—at least not without our catching on."

"But Gus?" He rubbed his forehead with two fingers. "How does she know him?"

"If she's been hanging around your condo, she's probably seen him."

"And how did she get him to go along with this?"

"Billy." She squeezed his shoulders and shook him. "You're not thinking like a cop. If this weren't Sabrina, you'd see it makes sense—and even if it doesn't, remember her message. Don't turn down any invitations. This is an invitation, plain and simple. You're not thinking clearly about this case. It's too personal. You're too close."

Or was his muddled thinking because he'd become too close to Mia? Had she compromised this case, her witness, by engaging with her witness's brother? Tucker probably had a point leaving Billy out of the equation. She'd used Billy's confrontation with Lawrence Coleman as a justification for her actions, blowing her cover and letting Billy in on his sister's predicament.

If she were honest with herself, she had just wanted to get on Billy's radar.

"You're right. God, you're right." Pinching the bridge of his nose, he squeezed his eyes shut. "I was just saying I'd be waiting around for an invitation, and when the first one comes my way, I can't even recognize it for what it is."

"It's because you're directly involved, Billy. That's why detectives and investigators and cops and agents and marshals recuse themselves from cases where they're personally affected. We wouldn't be able to do our jobs."

He took her hands. "Do you regret inviting me in?"

"I regret absolutely nothing." She brought their clasped hands to her lips and kissed his knuckles. "Let's get ready to set sail tonight."

"IT'LL WORK, TUCKER." Mia wedged her feet against the coffee table in her hotel room. "Nick still believes in her. She'll lead us right to him, and when she does, the Feds can pick him up."

"And Sabrina goes right back into WITSEC until Nick goes on trial and is convicted. Nothing the Carluccis can do at that point."

Mia puffed out a breath. "You know how long that can take. She's not gonna go for that."

"I don't care what she wants. That's the way it has to be."

"WITSEC is not a prison sentence, Tucker. We can't make people stay. She's already checked herself out." Mia ground her teeth together. There was no way Sabrina would agree to all this if she knew it was going to land her back in WITSEC.

Tucker coughed. "Don't forget. We have ways of making people cooperate."

Mia dropped her feet to the floor and dug her elbows into her knees. "You are not going to threaten that young woman. We have nothing on her."

"Maybe she knew about the hit in advance."

Mia could almost feel steam coming from her ears. "That's not right, Tucker, and you know it."

"What I do know is that you have permission to carry out this dangerous scheme only if the end result is reeling Sabrina back into the fold. You did your own sting operation under the guidance and protection of the FBI."

"Sabrina will have me and her brother. We'll call in the Feds when a meeting with Nick is imminent."

Tucker blew out a noisy breath. "That's another thing. You brought a civilian into our operation. I'm going to have to pretend I don't know anything about that."

"Billy Crouch is hardly a civilian. He's an LAPD homicide detective with almost fifteen years on the force and the best solve rate of any detective in the department."

"Such a passionate defense." Tucker cleared his throat.

Mia held her breath. She didn't need Tucker asking her any nosy questions. "I trust him."

"Obviously, but we both know personal attachments can muddy the waters of any operation."

She had no answer to that, as she'd just pointed that out to Billy this morning.

Tucker continued. "All you're going to do tonight is meet with Sabrina, right? We'll call in the FBI to map out next steps."

"I just don't think she's going to agree to that, Tucker. It's bad enough that I'm involved. Once we mention the FBI, she'll flee. It'll be all over, and we'll never get our hands on Nick Carlucci."

"We still have that guy in a Vegas hospital—Lawrence Coleman."

Mia's pulse jumped. "He's conscious?"

"Not yet, but when he gets there, maybe he can tell us something about Nick's whereabouts."

She swung her legs back up on the table and wiggled her toes. Tucker had nothing. "If Coleman didn't spill his guts about Nick while a Carlucci soldier had a knife to those very same guts, he doesn't know anything. He might know Nick's trying to find Sabrina for a happy reunion, but I doubt he knows where Nick is. Nope—Nick is gonna come out of hiding for Sabrina and Sabrina only. She's our key, and we have to play it her way."

"Whatever. Say what you have to say to get her to the point, and then we'll do what we have to do—to protect her and nail Nick Carlucci for the murder of Ray Mayberry."

"Copy that."

Tucker ended the call, and Mia cupped the phone in her hand, juggling it from one palm to the other. She copied, all right, but she had a feeling Sabrina had her own plans, and they'd have to roll with those if they wanted to get their handcuffs on Nick Carlucci.

Her phone buzzed, and she answered the call from Billy. "Anything new from Gus?"

"Haven't seen him—or anyone else near his boat this afternoon, although the boat two slips over is having a party. I suppose that's good cover for us to take off. What have you been doing?"

"Talked to Tucker." She sucked in her bottom lip.

Billy paused two beats. "And?"

"I told him about our proposed meeting with Sabrina tonight. He's on board—not literally, but you know what I mean."

"What does he hope to achieve from the meeting?"

"What we all hope—a bead on Nick Carlucci." She didn't need Billy asking any more questions. "I checked sunset tonight, and it's at seven fifty-two. Should we be down at the boat slip by seven?"

"I'm no sailor, but I suppose that will give us enough time to motor out of the marina and be on the open water by sunset. Even if that's not the purpose of the trip."

"It's not. Has Gus ever invited you on his boat before?"

"Negative."

"There you go." She glanced at the time. "I'm going to get ready. I'll meet you at your place in forty-five minutes. Hey, nothing on Coleman yet, is there?"

"Checked in after you left today. He's still out."

"Nothing from Beckett?"

"Wasn't expecting anything. I just hope he didn't rat us out to Nick."

Mia pushed up from the couch and wandered into the kitchen. "I don't think he'd want Nick to know that we questioned him. Beckett doesn't believe he gave us any useful information, so he's not going to believe we'll have any contact with Sabrina."

"Because he still thinks Sabrina and Nick are some star-crossed lovers destined to be together.

Mia snorted. "Beckett didn't strike me as much of a romantic."

"You never know. I'm going to get my gear together. I'll see you soon."

Mia tossed her phone on the bed and yanked open a dresser drawer. Billy was right about romance. You never did know. Who would've believed chasing after an errant witness would lead her to the greatest romance she'd ever experienced?

AT ABOUT FIFTEEN minutes to seven, the buzzer to Billy's condo sounded. He checked the video and let Mia into the building.

He had the door open for her when she stepped off the elevator all in black. He pointed to his chest, snug in a black tee. "Great minds think alike, but if Gus is really inviting us to a sunset cruise, he's going to question our odd fashion choices."

She strode toward him, her black Vans matching the rest of her outfit. Standing on tiptoes, she kissed his lips. "That's what I like about you, Crouch, always thinking about fashion."

He tugged on the strap of her backpack. "You have your piece?"

"Just in case. You bringing yours?"

"Don't leave home without it."

"Are you excited?" She patted his chest just over his thundering heart. "You finally get to see your sister."

"I'm beyond." He dug his fingers into the back of his neck.

"But?"

How had he and Mia gotten so attuned to each other in such a short time? She didn't miss a thing.

"I'm nervous. This is not like meeting her at the airport or even going to the hospital to collect her. This is some cloak-and-dagger stuff usually reserved for my job."

She traced her fingertip along his tight jaw. "It'll be okay. It's just a meeting. You can see with your own eyes that she's fine. Then we get to the hard part where she tells us how and where she's going to be meeting with Nick."

"She's going to tell us?"

"She has to. Your sister knows what she's doing. She's been able to evade the Feds, the Carluccis and her psycho ex-boyfriend." Mia rubbed his back.

"That doesn't make me feel any better."

"How about this?" She curled her arms around his neck and kissed his mouth, her soft lips moving against his.

He tugged on a lock of her wavy hair. "Under the right circumstances, your kiss could make me forget all my troubles."

"Beckett ain't got nothin' on you in the romance department."

He tipped his head back and laughed. He loved how she could turn any situation on its head. "Okay, partner. Let's go. You know I hate sailing, right?"

"Didn't know that. Seasickness and everything?"

"Not quite, but that's why it's unbelievable if not ironic that Sabrina would choose a boat."

"Your condo *is* right on the marina. Besides, it's brilliant. We can be sure we're not being trailed—or in the scope of a sniper on top of a building."

"Aren't you supposed to be calming my nerves?"

"Best way to calm a cop's nerves and to get him into the action." She grabbed his arm. "Let's go."

They walked down the metal dock to Gus's slip.

The party on the boat had wound down, and it looked like the remaining guests might set sail soon. Maybe they had the sunset on their minds, too.

Gus popped up on the deck of his boat when he heard their footsteps, his gray hair standing on end. "Welcome, welcome."

"Thanks for the invitation, Gus. This is Mia."

Gus extended his hand to Mia as both a greeting and an assist onto the boat. "Nice to meet you, Mia. It's the perfect night for a short trip. That little cloud cover should give us a colorful sunset, too."

She said, "It's been a while since I've been on a sailboat, but if you need any help, let us know what to do."

As he glanced at the stairs that led below deck, Billy licked his lips, salty from the sea. Was Sabrina down there? Was he minutes and feet away from seeing his sister?

He didn't ask and Gus didn't tell. Gus started the motor on the boat. Even Billy knew the sailboats had to motor in and out of the channels that led to the ocean, but that didn't mean the sailors couldn't hoist their sails.

Gus put them to work, and they raised the sails, which flapped in the breeze as the boat continued to chug out to sea, now a deep turquoise, which reminded him of Mia's eyes.

Once they cleared the channel, Gus engaged the sails in earnest and took a position behind the steering wheel. The ocean opened in front of them, dotted here and there with white sails, a gray oil tanker sitting way offshore. The party boat had the same idea and unfurled its sails as it left the channel.

Billy and Mia stood shoulder to shoulder, the salty breeze in their faces tossing Mia's hair. The water splashed beside them, and Mia jabbed his arm.

"Look! Two dolphins."

As Billy watched them frolic at the water's surface, his belly tied in knots thicker than the ropes on the boat, Gus said quietly, "Are you ready?"

Billy turned around, holding on to the boat's railing, his hand sweaty. His heart rattled against his rib cage as a woman emerged from below deck, her dark clothing hanging on her stooped frame, a hat pulled over her face. He'd seen her before—the homeless woman who haunted the boats.

When she reached the deck, she pulled off the hat and straightened to her full height. The beloved smile he remembered so well spread across her beautiful, if dirty, face. "Hey, brother."

Billy's throat closed, thick with tears and emotion. He ate up the space between him and Sabrina with two long strides and wrapped his arms around her. He buried his face in her wildly curly hair to staunch the tears that threatened to pour down his face.

He finally choked out, "Sabrina."

Her thin arms curled around him. "Billy, I'm so sorry."

Standing back from her, he wiped the corner of his eye. "You have nothing to apologize for. I'm so happy you're alive and safe. Mom is going to be over the moon."

One side of her mouth curled up. "One thing at a time. Right, Mia?"

"I'm glad you're alive, too, Chanel."

"Did you doubt me?" She shrugged out of the dirty coat flapping around her body. "And Chanel's gone—for good."

"The longer you stayed on the outside and kept out of sight, the less I doubted you… Sabrina." Mia tugged her own jacket tighter around her as the wind picked up. "You have a plan to reel in Nick. Let's hear it."

Billy held his breath as he held his sister's hand. If she told them she really wanted to be with Nick, he'd shatter into pieces on the deck of this boat.

"I do have a plan." Sabrina squeezed his hand and then dropped it as a buzzing sound came from somewhere in her voluminous clothing. She held up one finger. "Hold on. Let me get this. Unless it's spam, there's only one person who has this number."

Sabrina pulled the phone from her clothing and tapped the screen. Her eyes widened, making Billy's heart stutter.

"What's wrong?"

Gus shouted, "Hey, did someone bring this bag on board?"

As if in slow motion, Billy switched his gaze from Sabrina's shocked face to the black bag in Gus's hand. His eyes darted back to Sabrina as she held her phone out to show him Beckett's rearranged face.

Sabrina gasped. "They got him. They got to my contact."

Billy yelled, "Drop the bag, Gus."

Mia flew past him and grabbed Sabrina. "Off the boat! Everyone in the water."

Gus dropped the bag, and Billy yanked on his arm, pulling him toward the boat's edge. Mia and Sabrina had already jumped overboard, and Billy had to push Gus to get him to jump. He dived into the chilly water after him.

"Everybody, get away from the boat!"

Billy helped Gus as the two women streaked away faster than the dolphins. The four of them bobbed in the water well away from the sailboat that the wind had carried even farther away.

Mia coughed and sputtered. "Maybe…"

Billy didn't hear the rest of her words as Gus's sailboat exploded, shooting a ball of fire into the air that rivaled the sun finally dipping into the inky sea.

Chapter Seventeen

Mia closed her eyes against the ash that wafted toward them, the heat of the fire making the cold water seeping into her skin almost bearable.

Gus gurgled. "What the hell just happened?"

"Gus, I'm so sorry. I told you it would be dangerous." Sabrina still had her phone clasped in her hand. "They found Beckett. His face was all battered. They must've gotten him to talk."

The sailboat that had followed them out of the marina was making a beeline for them. Billy, hanging on to Gus, said, "The why and how can come later. We need to get out of this water, and help is on the way. I just hope they're sober enough to find us."

The sailors on the party boat were not only sober enough to find them; they were sober enough to rescue all four of them, take them back to the marina and call the Coast Guard.

Two hours later, Mia sat across from Billy and Sabrina nestled together on his couch, sipping hot coffee.

Cradling her own coffee, she said, "I'm just glad Gus has insurance on that boat."

"He was less devastated than I thought he'd be." Billy tousled Sabrina's curls. "I think he got a kick out of the excitement."

"Because he doesn't know what it all means." This time, Mia had dressed in Billy's T-shirt and a pair of his old sweats, but there was nothing sexy about it at all. They could've all died tonight.

Sabrina, whose long legs fit Billy's sweats better than hers did, curled one of the legs beneath her. "Beckett knew I was hanging out by the boats. He knew I was dressed as a transient. The Carluccis must've figured it out, gotten info on my contact with Gus. There are plenty of homeless people hanging around who would be more than happy to give up some information in exchange for money."

"At least they didn't get to you." Billy hooked his arm around his sister's neck and pulled her close.

Mia snapped her fingers. "It could've been someone on that party boat. You said Gus wasn't around this afternoon. It wouldn't have been too hard for someone to slip onto that boat during the festivities and plant that bomb. You were sleeping on Gus's boat, Sabrina?"

"I was." She nodded, her fine-boned face so similar to Billy's.

Billy said, "They might not have known about our meeting at all. Maybe they were just hoping to get Sabrina while she was sleeping on the boat."

Sabrina shivered, the first sign of fear Mia had seen on the girl all evening.

Billy set his cup on the coffee table and turned

Sabrina to face him. "How do we know this was the Carluccis and not one particular Carlucci?"

"I know it's not Nick." She wiggled her fingers in Billy's face. "Beckett is Nick's guy, and he tried to warn me."

"How can you be so sure?" Billy dug his fingers into his hair. "How can you trust him?"

Sabrina shrugged. "He loves me. You trust the person you love, no questions asked."

Mia squirmed under Sabrina's gaze as it shifted from her to Billy. "Am I right, Mia? Michael trusted you because he loved you."

Billy jerked his head up. "You told her about that?"

"You told him about that?" Sabrina jabbed a finger at her brother.

Mia raised her hands in surrender. "I told Sabrina about my past to show her I empathized with her situation—that she wasn't the only young woman with stars in her eyes to fall for a bad boy. I told your brother because…it just came up."

"Okay." Sabrina rolled her dark brown eyes. "I need to get in touch with Becket and find out if he's okay and what he told the Carluccis."

"Not a good idea." Billy sliced his hand through the air. "You move ahead with your plan to meet Nick. You don't need Beckett. Are you communicating with Nick through Castles and Crosses?"

"How did you two know about that gaming site? I almost fell over when I saw Cool Breeze moving through the rooms and messaging me."

"That was Mia's brilliance." Billy jerked his thumb at Mia.

"I knew it couldn't be you." Sabrina smacked her brother's leg. "Unless those nephews of mine got you hooked."

"They play some games, but not that one." Billy wiped his brow. "That one is for mature audiences only—or should be."

"Any parents who let their kids on Castles and Crosses need their heads examined." Sabrina scrunched her curls, still damp from the ocean. "Nick and I are still using it to communicate. I'm going to contact him and let him know what his family tried to do. Any talk of his family coming after me only draws Nick closer to me. He'll be livid, and it will give me the opportunity to suggest meeting in person, if he's ready."

Mia tipped her head to the side. "Has he not been ready?"

"He's been planning, but he's close. This latest incident will push him over the edge, spur him on. I've just been waiting for the chance to set him up. With you two on board, we can nail him."

Billy hunched forward. "Let's talk a minute about what's going to happen during the setup. You'll agree to meet him somewhere so the two of you can take off together, but the FBI will be waiting for him instead and take him into custody."

"Oh, no." Sabrina smacked the coffee table, rattling the cups. "No FBI. Is that why Mia's involved? To bring in the rest of the Feds? I won't go through with it if the Feds are there. I'm not going back, Mia. I'm done with Chanel."

Mia clasped her hands between her knees. She'd warned Tucker about this. "Maybe we can arrest Nick on our own."

Billy asked, "But then what? You will still have to wait to testify against Nick before you're out of danger. If the Carluccis get to you before or during the trial, Nick skates free. You're not safe until after the trial, Sabrina."

Sabrina's pretty face hardened and her eyes glittered. "I can handle it."

Mia shot a worried glance at Billy. What was Sabrina planning? "You mean, you're going to live as Sabrina Crouch in LA while waiting to testify against a mob son in a murder trial?"

The corner of Sabrina's eye twitched. "I said I can handle it."

"Sabrina…"

Sabrina bounced from the couch, putting distance between her and her brother. "It happens my way, or it doesn't happen at all. For once, I'm holding all the cards. I can give you Nick Carlucci, but in exchange, I get Sabrina Crouch back. That's the deal."

The former Sabrina with the romantic ideals and the obedient, grateful Chanel stood before them with her nostrils flaring, eyes blazing and lips pressed into a hard line.

Mia believed her, all right. She just wasn't all that sure about Sabrina's plan.

"You're right." Billy stood up and hugged Sabrina's

stiff frame. "You call the shots. Get that meeting set up with Nick, and we'll be your support."

"Here?" Mia gestured toward the balcony over the boat slips. "Do you think we're safe?"

"With all this…" Billy nudged his toe against the kitchen table loaded with an arsenal big enough to take down a small government. "We can hold off anyone. I'll be on watch tonight, monitoring the cameras."

Mia said, "You mean you're taking first shift. We all need to get some sleep. You most of all, Sabrina."

"After I do some gaming." She positioned herself on the couch again, Billy's laptop on her thighs. She navigated to the game and used her own log-in to start playing.

Billy asked Mia if she wanted more coffee and went into the kitchen with both their mugs. As he poured, he asked Sabrina, "Did you even know Lawrence Coleman?"

"Lawrence was Nick's friend from high school. Got into dealing drugs and thought his connection to Nick could catapult his career." She clicked the mouse and sighed. "It's so much easier to play on a TV with a gaming system. That's the first thing I'm going to buy James and Darius when I get settled."

Billy snorted. "Coleman got catapulted, all right. Did he know where Nick was?"

Sabrina answered, "In the beginning, but Nick moved on from that location. He didn't want his family to know he was trying to contact me."

"And Bri? Did you know her?" Billy handed Mia her coffee.

"Didn't know her until Beckett told me to look out for her—which I did. I looked out for her and stayed away, but I'm sorry she got mixed up in this. I'm sorry for everyone." She raised her shimmering eyes to Billy. "I'm sorry I missed Pop."

"He'd be proud of you for doing the right thing, Stick." Billy squeezed Mia's shoulder. "Do you want to help me set up the boys' room for Sabrina?"

Billy kept his sons' room immaculate and ready for anything, but as she opened her mouth to reply, he squeezed harder. "Yeah, sure. Let's get that ready while she tries to get on Nick's radar."

Mia followed Billy into the guest bedroom with the bunk beds neatly made up with matching outer space–themed bedspreads.

He pulled the door closed and folded her into his arms. "What do you think she's up to? She can't possibly think she can live as a transient for the few years it may take to try and convict Nick."

Mia lifted her shoulders. "I'm not sure. Maybe she thinks she can convince Nick to confess. That way, she doesn't even have to testify, and his family will back off. If he loves her as much as she thinks he does, that might not be a stretch."

"He might love her—up until the minute he realizes she set him up and doesn't actually want to run away with him. A man scorned isn't a pretty prospect. How did Michael Guardino react?"

Mia dipped her head, allowing her damp hair to shield her face. "He was hurt. I never spoke to him again."

"Nick might be more than hurt."

"Let's see how it plays out. We have to give her a chance. We don't have a choice right now."

Sabrina squealed from the other room, and Billy lunged for the door with Mia hot on his heels. "What's wrong?"

"Wrong?" She looked up from the computer. "Nothing's wrong. Everything's right. I made contact with Nick and he's ready to go...tonight."

"Tonight?" Mia pressed a hand to her chest.

"You mean morning. We're almost past midnight now."

"Even better." Sabrina flexed her fingers. "I'm more than ready."

"What's his plan?" Billy sat beside Sabrina on the couch and looked over her shoulder.

"A boat, of course. It was perfect for Gus, and it's perfect now."

"Uh, in case you forgot—" Mia lifted a strand of her own damp hair "—that was not perfect."

"This is Nick's own boat. He'll make sure nobody gets on it or puts anything on it. He plans to sail it all the way down to Mexico."

Billy clasped his hands on top of his head. "How are we going to get on it?"

Sabrina waved a hand in the air, as if Billy had mentioned a minor point. "Oh, you can figure that out."

Mia bit her bottom lip. "Could we follow in an inflatable? It'll be dark enough. They don't make much noise. If we could keep to one side of the boat, and

Sabrina keeps him on the other side. If you could get him below deck at some point, we could board."

"Even if you rushed in with a power boat, what's Nick going to do at that point?" Sabrina flicked back a curl.

"He could take you hostage at gunpoint. Then we'd have to back off, and he'd know you set him up." Billy massaged his temples.

"He'll never know I set him up." Sabrina set her jaw. "He might even think you're from the family."

"Scuba." Mia sat on the edge of the coffee table. "You're certified, aren't you, Billy? And I can dive."

"How'd you know I—" He shook his head. "Never mind. Where are we going to get scuba gear at this time of the morning?"

"There's a scuba shop where they give instruction up from the slips. We can break in there and get all our gear." Mia shrugged. "We'll give it all back."

"I suppose that can work. We follow in an inflatable and then leave it and approach underwater. Sabrina, you're going to have to make him go slow or stop or do something to the sails. We can't swim underwater and catch up to a sailboat." Billy's tone indicated that he thought his sister could do all of the above.

"I'll handle things on my end, and you handle things on yours." She clapped. "Let's get going. We have a lot to do before we go on our second boat ride in twenty-four hours. Let's just hope this one has a happier ending."

Mia and Billy dashed around the condo to get

ready as Sabrina serenely donned her dry homeless garb. She insisted on leaving earlier than them and gave her brother a kiss on the cheek and even hugged Mia before she slipped back into the shadows.

As they collected their weapons, which Mia assured Billy they could conceal in a waterproof bag, she peered under the coffee table and felt beneath the couch.

Billy checked a cartridge and snapped it into place. "What's wrong?"

Sabrina's mouth went dry as she pulled out the cushions of the couch.

Billy's brow creased. "What are you looking for?"

Mia licked her lips. "I know what Sabrina's plan is—and it's a surefire one."

"What are you talking about?"

Mia locked eyes with Billy and said, "She's going to kill him."

Chapter Eighteen

Despite what Mia had read about him, Billy hadn't been diving in years. As they loaded the equipment into the inflatable, he examined some of the newfangled gadgets and vowed to take it up again.

He couldn't get his mind around Mia's belief that Sabrina planned to shoot Nick herself. She'd taken the gun from their stash for protection. That's all. She'd play by the rules and let them take him down. Sabrina had always played by the rules.

He tapped Mia on the arm. The tracker she'd slipped onto Sabrina had started moving. "She's heading for Nick's boat."

Mia sealed a gun into a waterproof pouch and stashed it onto their vessel. "Keep an eye on her, and we'll maneuver toward his slip."

Billy eyed the display on Mia's phone. "Looks like it's down on the end, away from Gus's slip. We may have to wait until they take off before heading over. We don't want him—or anyone else—to hear us."

"We can't wait too long. I'm telling you, Billy. That's why Sabrina didn't care how we got out there.

That's why she's not concerned about staying safe during the trial. There's not going to be a trial. She's going to take him out—problem solved."

"She can't do that, Mia. She's going to open up a whole new set of problems for herself. You can't run around killing people, even if they are on the FBI's most-wanted list. I just don't believe she could do it."

"You don't know your sister, Billy. We need to get to that boat ASAP."

He squinted at the phone. "She's stationary. She's on the boat."

"Hopefully, they're having a happy reunion, and Sabrina is everything Nick has imagined her to be all these years."

Billy climbed into the boat beside Mia as she pushed off. "What if he finds the gun? What if his plan all along was to kill her?"

"Even more reason we need to get out to that boat."

They were able to creep along the channel, darting among the boat slips, closer and closer to Nick's sailboat.

They bumped into a larger boat as Mia jerked on the steering wheel. "There they go."

Billy let out a breath. "I didn't hear any gunshots. Everything must be going according to plan."

Mia mumbled, "That's what I'm worried about."

As they watched the boat break free from the channel lane, Billy said, "He doesn't look as skilled as Gus. He's not going very fast."

"That's a good thing, although how he thinks he's

going to sail down to Mexico on a boat that size is beyond me."

"Obviously, the guy dreams big."

They followed Nick's boat at a safe distance, but not too far, as they'd still have to swim to it. The current was working in their direction, and the sea was calm, as if nature had conspired to give Sabrina the break she finally needed and deserved.

They'd already slipped into their wetsuits, and their tanks, belts, weights and fins awaited them.

Mia grabbed his arm. "They're faltering. I don't know if that's Nick's poor sailing skills or Sabrina's machinations. Let's keep getting as close as possible. If we had a light on our boat and he was bothering to look out this way, he'd see us."

"Sabrina is too confident that Nick won't hurt her. If he's such a romantic and she betrays him, he just might set it up to look like a Romeo and Juliet double suicide." Billy grabbed his tank with more force than he intended and knocked into Mia's gear. "Sorry."

"It's all right. Calm down. We can do this. The boat has stopped completely. One of the sails is going wonky. Nick's going to be occupied with it."

Billy sweated in his wetsuit as he struggled with his tank. Then he helped Mia with hers. They attached their waterproof pouches containing their guns to their belts and slipped into the water.

They swam for what seemed forever, every few minutes, one of them popping their head up to keep track of the boat, which bobbed on the swells, its sails flat.

The next time Mia broke the surface, she came back down giving him a thumbs-up. She didn't have to tell him. He could see the bottom of the boat beneath the waterline. He just hoped to God both Nick and Sabrina were still alive when they got there.

They both paddled to the surface and tipped their heads back, listening. The water slapped against the sides of the boat, and the sails smacked back and forth uselessly. But Billy couldn't hear much else.

He followed Mia to the back of the boat, where a silver ladder clung to the side. Mia hung on to the ladder and shed her tank, belt and fins, letting them float on the water.

He sure as hell hoped they had another way off this boat when the dust…or the gunfire settled.

As she reached the deck, Mia cranked her head over her shoulder and put her finger to her lips.

She didn't have to tell him to keep quiet, or maybe she could hear his heart hammering in his chest. He sloughed off his gear like a second skin and climbed the ladder.

He froze when the sea breeze carried a man's voice across the air. "I can fix it, Sabrina. Don't worry. I know what I'm doing."

Billy swallowed, salt water and all. Nick was still alive—and so was Sabrina.

Mia crouched before him, yanking her pouch from the belt and fishing out her weapon. This woman had nerves of steel.

Billy followed suit. The flapping sails drowned out Sabrina's answer to Nick and their stealthy movements on the boat. Did Sabrina even know they were here? Did she care?

Suddenly, Sabrina's voice cut through the background noise. "It's over, Nick."

Billy almost dropped his weapon. Mia had been right. They had to stop Sabrina.

Mia peered around the corner, and before he could take the lead, she stepped out, her gun pointed in front of her.

"Nick Carlucci, you're under arrest for the murder of Ray Mayberry. Get down on the deck."

Billy stepped into the open, his gaze darting from Nick, his eyes wide and his mouth open, to Sabrina, still in her transient garb aiming her weapon at Nick as steadily as Mia was.

Billy said, "Sabrina, you can put down that gun. We'll handle it from here."

"Handle it?" Sabrina's sharp laugh hurt his ears. "Like I'm supposed to live some other life as some other person while a trial drags on? No. This ends here and now."

Billy almost felt sorry for the handsome young man with the movie-star features and wavy black hair as he held out one hand pleadingly. "Sabrina, what are you doing? We're going to be together. Just you and me. I'll protect you from my family. Didn't I at the very beginning? I knew what they would've expected from me when I realized you saw everything. But I couldn't do that to you, Sabrina. I love you."

"Love me?" Sabrina choked out a sob. "How could

you bring me into that world? How could you kill that man? You ruined my life."

"I never meant... I wanted to leave the family, Sabrina. Even more after I met you. We talked about family expectations all the time. Remember our chats?"

"Yeah, we talked about family expectations, but my family's expectations never included murder. I'm sorry, Nick. I have to be free, and this is the only way."

Mia shouted, "It's not, Sabrina. We can protect you. This is not the way. Your brother and I, we can't cover this up."

Sabrina sniffled. "I'm sorry, Billy. I'm sorry I disappointed you in so many ways, but I want my life back."

As the drama unfolded in front of him and Billy prayed for his sister to see sense, he heard a grumbling roar in the distance. He glanced to the side, the dark water stretching out before him except for a white line of foam heading their way.

He shouted, "Sabrina, get down. Mia, drop!"

The other three on the boat slowly woke up to the grumbling noise approaching them from the darkness.

Mia dropped to the deck, her gun still positioned in front of her.

Sabrina turned her head toward the sound, her mouth dropping open.

Without looking behind him, Billy dived for Sabrina and tackled her to the deck, holding his weapon aloft.

Light flooded the boat and a single shot rang out. Nick's body jumped, and then he fell back.

Mia rolled onto her stomach and braced her gun on the edge of the boat, squeezing off two shots of her own.

The sailboat went dark again, and the powerboat that had descended on them sped off toward open water.

Sabrina's scream rose over the whispering sails that had seemed to go silent. Sobbing, she crawled toward Nick's still form, blood spreading out from the back of his head.

Billy slumped against the side of the boat. Sabrina had gotten her wish courtesy of the Carlucci family—freedom.

Epilogue

Darius tugged on Sabrina's sleeve. "Auntie Sabrina, you said you'd take us to look at the boats."

Billy raised his eyebrows at his sister, her dark curls brushing her shoulders, a new—but different—light in her eyes. "I think Auntie Sabrina has had enough of boats for a while."

She giggled, and that sound was the same as it ever was. "A promise is a promise."

James untangled his long legs and jumped to her side. "You also promised you'd make sure Dad got us an Xbox before you left to see Nana."

"You're gonna hold your auntie to all those promises she made when she first laid eyes on you?" Billy clicked his tongue.

"Boats first." She held out her hand to Darius, who grabbed it.

Mia called from the kitchen, "And then you're all coming back here for lunch. Your dad said you guys like your sandwiches with chips crushed on them, and I got the chips."

James stopped on his way out the front door and

peered at Mia shyly through lowered eyelashes. "Thanks, Mia."

The boys had met Mia last week for the first time, two weeks after the shoot-out on the boat, and they'd sensed something different. Billy had never introduced his sons to a girlfriend before, so this was uncharted territory for everyone.

"Hey, hey." Billy snapped his fingers. "Say goodbye to J-Mac and Kyra. They'll probably be gone before you get back."

Darius dropped Sabrina's hand and rushed back to Jake and Kyra, throwing his arms around Kyra's waist. James followed his brother at a more sedate pace and fist-bumped with Jake.

Then Jake gave Sabrina a long hug. "It's good to have you back, kiddo. You sure you want to continue as an accountant? The way you handled yourself, you'd be an asset to the department."

"Ugh, those days are over for me. I have a date with a nice, normal computer geek tomorrow."

Billy jerked his head up. "Computer geek? You don't mean Brandon Nguyen, do you?"

"Of course. I want to stick with guys I meet in person. I'm done with dating apps for a while."

Kyra winked at her. "I think your brother is, too."

Sabrina gathered up the boys again and took them outside into the sunshine.

Shaking his head, Jake said, "I can't believe I missed all the excitement."

"Excuse me?" Kyra nudged him. "You were on your honeymoon with me."

"Ooh, brother." Billy punched his partner in the arm. "You need to watch yourself now. You're a married man."

Mia came in from the kitchen with lemonade refills for everyone. "That was probably the most harrowing assignment I've ever had."

Kyra glanced between Mia and Billy, a small smile on her lips. "Did the Marshal Service reprimand you for going rogue, Mia?"

Mia perched on the arm of Billy's chair. "I did get written up, but not suspended. We lost the suspect but saved the witness. In the end, that counted for a lot."

Jake asked, "Did that guy in Vegas ever come out of it?"

"Lawrence Coleman. He did." Billy clinked the ice in his glass. "Turns out he didn't know anything about Nick's whereabouts, but he's going to be on the Carluccis' bad list from now on. Mia's department is trying to get him to rat out the family and go into WITSEC."

Mia said, "Beckett, who was working with Nick, has already taken us up on our offer to relocate him."

"I don't wanna rain on the parade or anything—" Jake cleared his throat "—but is Sabrina in the clear with the Carluccis?"

Mia rested her hand on the back of Billy's neck. "Absolutely. She didn't know any of the family's secrets, didn't even know Nick was in the mob. She only had evidence of Ray-May's murder, didn't even know why Nick killed him. The Carluccis are done with her. They took care of their problem themselves."

Kyra shivered. "Imagine killing your own family member like that."

Billy and Mia said at the same time, "Fredo."

"What?" Kyra tipped her head.

"I'll explain it in the car." Jake put down his glass and took Kyra's hand. "We'd better get going, but let's do this again—barbecue and everything at my place, or a Dodgers game."

"Wait." Kyra pulled her husband up from the couch, both hands on his. "Doesn't Mia live in DC?"

Jake kissed the side of her head. "You are so behind. I'll explain that in the car, too."

At the door, as Mia told Kyra she was putting in for a transfer to LA, Jake grabbed Billy's shoulder and squeezed. "Brother, I'm so happy for you—not just that Sabrina's home and safe, but you seem to have found yourself a woman who gets you, even more than I do."

"I think *she* found *me*." He pounded Jake on the back...because they never hugged.

When they closed the door on the newlyweds, Mia hooked her arms around his neck. "Whew. I think your partner and his wife like me even though I crashed their wedding. Your boys seem to tolerate me so far, and your sister has come around."

Rubbing her arms, he said, "You seem more concerned about them than me."

"Oh, I know *you* like me." She planted a kiss on the side of his neck.

"I more than like you, Molly—I mean, Mia."

She nipped at his collarbone with her teeth. "I sort

of suspected that, Cool Breeze, but you've never actually told me."

"I think I need to remedy that." He crushed her to his chest and whispered into her hair, "I love you, Mia Romano."

And with his heart full and his eyes clear, he'd never meant it more than anything in his life.

* * * * *

Don't miss the previous books in Carol Ericson's The Lost Girls miniseries:

Canyon Crime Scene
Lakeside Mystery
Dockside Danger

Available now wherever Harlequin Intrigue books are sold!

HARLEQUIN
PLUS

Try the best multimedia
subscription service for romance
readers like you!

Read, Watch and Play.

Experience the easiest way to get
the romance content you crave.

Start your **FREE TRIAL** at
<u>www.harlequinplus.com/freetrial</u>.